THE ANSWER TO EVERYTHING

THE
ANSWER
TO
EVERYTHING

Elyse Friedman

Patrick Crean Editions
An imprint of HarperCollins*PublishersLtd*

Published by Patrick Crean Editions, an imprint of HarperCollins Publishers Ltd

First edition

HarperCollins books may be purchased for educational, business,
or sales promotional use through our Special Markets Department.

HarperCollins Publishers Ltd
2 Bloor Street East, 20th Floor
Toronto, Ontario, Canada
M4W 1A8

www.harpercollins.ca

Library and Archives Canada Cataloguing in Publication
information is available upon request

ISBN 978-1-44342-915-3

Printed and bound in the United States of America
RRD 9 8 7 6 5 4 3 2 1

To Daphne Floros and Max Friedman-Cole

Griffin

I needed a story. Something local, but juicy. And more than just newsworthy. I was holding out for gasp-worthy.

And I found it. Or rather, it found me. Yup, your humble J-school grad was pretty much handed a tale that had it all: sex and drugs (not the regular kinds), multiple deaths (untimely, natch), rich folks and rituals and loads o' lawsuits—even a celebrity cherry on top.

My newbie journo peers might be settling for three inches of coyotes in the subway, some spry centenarian's weightlifting regime or a bucket of campylobacter in the church supper salad, but I was planning to debut large and with oomph.

The story was mine.

I just had to figure out how to tell it.

PART I

PART 1

John

Why? That's what they keep asking me. As if it matters, as if *why* changes anything. I don't respond when they ask that. I don't say a word. I'm taking a page from Eldrich. *Don't you care about those individuals, Mr. Aarons? Don't you feel responsible?* I feel sad, I say. It's too bad, I say. All those people.

Answer me this: If a fool steers their Carrera into oncoming traffic, is Porsche responsible? Is Jägermeister responsible for the frat boy frozen in the snowbank? You make a product available. You can't be held accountable for how it gets used. Farmer Jones grew a lovely fat zucchini. Does that make him responsible for some idiot's perforated emergency-room rectum?

The world is full of humans, some of them good, most of them rotten (or rotten under the right circumstances). There are approximately 360,000 new ones each day. Plenty to go around, if you ask me. A very successful virus, if you'd like to know what I really think. Seven billion parasites, blindly, almost gleefully, defiling their host.

But back to the why of it all. I can't speak for others. I was out of the Institute at the end (luckily, according to the attorneys). I can't say why Eldrich did what he did. It was definitely counterproductive. Mystifying. Absurd. But I stopped understanding Eldrich a long time ago. I have no idea why those people chose the path they chose. I suppose that on a case-by-case basis I could formulate theories—this one's alky father/harelip/abortion, that one's war-torn native land . . .

As for Amy, well, I'll keep my opinions to myself for now. When it comes to the big why—why I started it all in the first place—I've been advised not to say anything just yet. When I am obliged to speak, I'm going to state plainly that I was trying to help people—that I wanted to connect with fellow Seekers who were curious about more than Brad Pitt's offspring or how much the markets had risen or fallen on any particular day. That's what I plan to say. I'm going to raise my right hand and swear an oath on the bible and say something just like that. It won't hurt that Eldrich believes me, and that Amy will claim she does. It's not like she can admit otherwise. So I'm confident I'll be in the clear.

Here's what I'm not going to do. I am not going to tell that old joke about the dog. Do you know it? Question: *Why does a dog lick his balls?* Answer: *Because he can.*

Eldrich

I knew from the beginning. I've always known, in the marrow of the marrow of my bones. God is. Grand. Great. Mysterious. A beautiful Rorschach of happiness for all humankind. If you open yourself to the light, you will receive it. Think of a flower blooming in time-lapse. Think of a fist relaxing and turning, making itself ready to accept.

God first visited me in the form of a bumblebee. Heavy yellow. A warm buzz in the mouth. It is my earliest memory. My mother told it always like this: *It was a humid afternoon and we were out in the yard. We didn't have air conditioning back then. Eldrich was about two and a half. He was playing in the sprinkler with a couple of neighbourhood kids—Sergio and Anthony from next door, and Patricia, who I used to babysit. Anyway, Eldrich toddled off, wandered into the garden and just plopped himself down in the middle of the daisies. I was going to fish him out, when I saw him pick up a bumblebee—he just scooped it right up and popped it in his mouth! I almost died! You know his father was allergic to bees? I screamed and went for him, but before I could get there his little mouth opened and the bee just flew out. It kind of bounced off a couple of flowers, and then lifted up and away. It didn't even sting him. And it was huge. The biggest bee I've ever seen! I just grabbed Eldrich and held him. I swear I almost died.*

Here's what I remember: everything is yellow and bright and shiny. The world vibrates with colour and shine. It's like a cartoon, but more vivid. You know when sun sparkles in blue pool water? The whole world was like that. Undulating and connected. Jell-O world. Illuminated from behind. God finds me in it. God feels that I am special. I am happy. I am happier than I have ever been. I open myself up, get the yellow inside me. The buzz of life in my mouth. Now I'm being lifted and twirled. It's Mother. It's sky. It's Mother. Sky. It's blue blue and white cloud.

My first real taste.

Amy

If it hadn't been for inconsiderate slobs in the laundry room, none of this would have happened. If it hadn't been for brown eyes and curly hair and the initial irresistibility of a certain acerbic asshole . . .

The first time I saw John Aarons was in a photograph. The Fine Arts Department was having its year-end exhibit, and I had wandered in to check it out on my lunch break. Visual Arts had taken over the Janine & Jeremy Goldstein Hall with a combination painting, drawing and photography show. Most of the stuff was crap—clunky or derivative. There were maybe a few items that fell into the technically-competent-but-totally-uninspired category. And then his installation, the only thing that showed any originality at all.

According to the artist's statement, he'd been working on it since the idea came to him when he was thirteen years old, on vacation with his parents. It was a series of photographs of people taking photographs of people in front of the world's most famous landmarks and tourist sites. He had taken hundreds of pictures of people taking pictures of people in front of Niagara Falls, the Hoover Dam, the Golden Gate Bridge and many other familiar spots. He claimed to have worked an entire year on a paper route in order to save enough money to fly to Egypt to take photos of people taking photos of people in front of the pyramids. I thought it was interesting. In a simple way it seemed to say a lot about our relationship with awe and mystery. And it was fascinating to see how sometimes the landmark in the background seemed cheapened by the tourists posing in front of it, and how sometimes the dignity and power of the thing seemed magnified. I thought it was pretty great, especially for a student piece. It was the only exhibit I lingered in front of and the only artist's statement I made it all the way through that day—a straightforward description of the project, mercifully free of art speak. There was a small portrait at the bottom, a selfie that showed a cute young guy with a sly smile—eyes hidden behind vintage Ray-Bans.

It was taken in front of the Sphinx.

Come
Come to me now
And rest
You are tired
So tired
A bird with no shore
A wheel turning and turning
Your struggle has not been worthwhile
But it will be worthwhile
The fruit can be yours
But you must first plant the seed
Come to me now
Begin

theanswertoeverything.org

John

"To live without meaning is the greatest challenge and the highest art." Who said that? Was it Sartre? Spinoza? Whoever dreamed it up, I think he may have been mistaken. I've had no trouble living without meaning. Living without money, on the other hand, has tested my mettle over the years. I am a resourceful type, though, and have always managed to fill my belly.

Art openings were a good bet. The fancier the gallery, the finer the spread. But even tiny joints on Queen Street would cube up some Costco cheddar and dump a box of Triscuits on a plate. You ingest a pound of cheese, it'll carry you through to the next morning. Book launches were also a solid source of nutrition and absurdly frequent—at least three a week once you got on the right mailing lists. You sometimes had to endure live readings by obscure/windy authors, but if you timed it right, not so much. I once dined modestly for several days on foodstuffs pilfered from a buffet table in the Reference Library during the Toronto Book Awards ceremony. While the crowd listened to our deputy mayor intone on matters civic, I filled my ironic, 100 percent plastic "Ceci n'est pas une plastic bag" bag with a half-tray of vegetarian sushi, a monstrous brie wedge and enough fresh broccoli florets to steam for dinner that night (thank you, authors who set their stories in Toronto).

In the afternoon, I often sampled my way through Whole Foods—a few grapes or cherries here, a handful or three of bulk cashews there. Customer Appreciation Day at the various big banks or Seniors Day at the drugstore yielded coffee and cake or cookies. I'll never forget this one grey granny giving me the hairy eyeball and waving a palsied digit in reprimand as I sword-swallowed a row of Arrowroot biscuits by the blood pressure monitor.

Open houses were reliably fruitful. While the real estate–mad inhabitants of Toronto checked out the coffered ceilings, front-loading washer-dryer and other features and finishes, I was checking out (and helping myself to) the contents of the stainless-steel refrigerator.

In summer, I ate locally and organically, harvesting veggie riches from various backyard and community gardens. And I found the rooftop bar at the Park Hyatt to be a very pleasant place. They served trays of premium toasted almonds, spicy olives and dried plantain, which you could inhale while waiting for your elusive friend, who never arrived. I'd use that tactic at restaurants too, downing a basket of bread and butter or, if I was lucky, humus, while repeatedly checking my watch and glancing anxiously at the door whenever somebody entered. When the carbs had been consumed, I would receive a call on my cell phone (my ex's, defunct, battery dead) indicating some kind of emergency and quickly mutter my harried apologies to the server as I swept past and out. When all else failed I invoked the old standby of inviting a flush friend out for a meal, dropping hints of impecuniousness during the repast and then high-tailing it to the bathroom as the cheque arrived.

Yes, there was an art to finding food and staying nourished. And I had no trouble mastering it. Rent, on the other hand, was a whole other matter.

Amy

The first time I saw John Aarons in the flesh was about five months after finding the exhibit in the Fine Arts Department. I was pretty sure it was him. He audited one of the classes I was in, a lecture on group influence and persuasion. I recognized the curly hair and the square jaw and the sly smile—he smiled a lot during the class and doodled spirographically on his white Converse sneakers while the rest of us took notes.

A week later, he turned up for Memory and Cognition. He was wearing a T-shirt that had "Eat More Cake" written on the front, and baby-blue, cockroach-killer cowboy boots. I tried to find him in the halls after class, but he had bolted. I started casually looking for him in the Arts wing. I'd eat lunch over there or take the long way to the bus stop, but I never ran into him.

Around that time I started sleeping with Ryan, my Statistics TA, and forgot about John for a while. Still, at the end of the year I made a point of attending the big Fine Arts exhibit opening-night party. He wasn't there and had nothing on display. I asked one of the profs, and she said he had dropped out halfway through the year—she seemed kind of drunk, and when pressed, let it slip that it had something to do with a series of bounced tuition cheques. I'm not quite sure why, but this piqued my interest in him more; maybe because I was bored and done with Ryan at that point. I Googled his name but got nothing relevant. There was no sign of him on Twitter/Vine/Vimeo, and while there was one "John Aarons" on Facebook, the listing was inactive—no profile picture and no Facebook friends. I figured I had seen the last of him.

If only!

Eldrich

I liked to watch the girls play. Philomena, Debbie, Gabriella, Jane. They lived on my street, and I would watch them do their hopscotch and gymnastics and skipping. I would watch them act out scenes with their Barbie dolls. They would fill a Tupperware container with water and the Barbies would have a pool party. Sometimes the girls played a game where they'd hold hands and dance around in a circle, singing a chant about flowers: *Apple blossom, almond blossom, fuchsia and azalea* . . .

One day a new girl came to play. Her name was Nikita. She was six years old but at least half a foot taller than the other girls who were the same age. She had a big head, a long neck and the skinniest legs I'd ever seen. Like a newborn colt's legs, barely able to support the weight of the body. Nikita did gymnastics with the others and everything seemed all right, but when the girls started to form a circle for the flower chant, she began to cry. She was on the sidewalk, sobbing, while the other girls stood in a circle on the lawn.

"What's going on?" I said. I was ten years old and bigger than them.

"They won't let me play," said Nikita.

"Why won't you let her play?" I asked the others.

Debbie said her parents told her not to touch black people. Philomena said her parents told her black people were bad.

"It's not true," I said. "Your parents are wrong."

The girls were shocked to hear this. Parents could be wrong?

"They're wrong," I said. "Nikita's skin is just a different colour than yours. How would you feel if the other girls wouldn't let you play because you had green eyes?" I asked Philomena. "How would you feel," I asked Debbie, "if the other girls wouldn't let you play because of that large brown mole on your shin?"

I brought Nikita into the circle. The girls joined hands and started doing the flower chant. They were instantly happy and smiling again. Just like that, every one of them having perfect afternoon fun. I stood in the centre of the circle and watched them. *Apple blossom, almond blossom, fuchsia and azalea . . . baby's breath and hollyhock, gardenia and camellia . . .* Faster and faster they went, chanting the names of the beautiful flowers—smiling faces spinning around me, faster and faster, an orbit of pretty—until they collapsed on the grass, all laughing and tangled, a kaleidoscope of happiness and relief.

I learned something that day. I learned that people sometimes need guidance. A small nudge in the direction of holy.

John

What ever happened to quiet desperation? All the bleating that goes on these days. I swear it makes my cochleas cringe.

When the ex turfed me out of our apartment (one that I'd found but had her fully employed, office-worker name on the lease), I didn't write a memoir about it, I got busy trying to locate a place to live. I couldn't afford anything on my own, so I had to look for shared accommodation. As far as I was concerned, there were only two options for potential room-mates—gay males or straight females. Individuals from either of these subsets were far more likely to clean up after themselves, and perhaps even after me if I was lucky. They would never use flags as curtains and wouldn't be slobbing around, watching sports all the time, trying to engage me in conversations about baseball or hockey or that most mystifying of pursuits, football. They would consistently have food in the fridge, and quality food too—butter (possibly organic) and premium, not-from-concentrate orange juice. None of those hetero male tubs of margarine and jumbo jugs of SunnyD crapola. More important, if I was charming enough, they would likely share their food with me, or at the very least not give me hell for pinching a pot of coffee or a bowl of cereal now and again.

Lesbians had good food too, but they tended toward vegetarianism (I need my meat) and usually chose female roommates. They were also savvy and man-wary and weren't likely to put up with my crap.

Anything over $850 per month was out of the question. Anything north of Eglinton, west of High Park or east of Greenwood was out of the question. Any habitation with the owner living on-site or within a half-mile radius was out of the question.

It took about six days to find a handful of viable options and narrow the field to three candidates. There was Vickie, twenty-something, associate producer at CBC Radio, in a flat on the second floor of a house near Pape and Danforth. Good restaurants, shopping and subway nearby. Hardwood floors, dishwasher and a claw-footed tub that had recently been reglazed. Seven hundred and forty dollars per month plus half the cable. Not bad. No outdoor space, though. And Vickie was a very unattractive girl. On the one hand, this was a plus. Vickie would be less likely to bring home romantic partners, who would clutter up the space and use all the hot soaking-tub water. On the other hand, ugly Vickie might be at home every night, filling the couch with methane and dust mites, watching *Long Island Medium* or *Cake Boss* marathons on TLC. Vickie clearly wasn't comfortable in her own, alarmingly oily, skin. The day I toured the apartment she wore a voluminous sweatshirt in an effort to hide her protruding belly and watermelon breasts. Because of my interest in social psychology, I knew that recent studies had shown that low self-esteem inhibits generosity and helpful behaviour. I required a generous and helpful roommate.

There was handsome Hal, an affable, twenty-something gay man who had a small, well-appointed condo to share on Hayden Street. The location was great, and the suite was decorated tastefully—all creamy natural colours, and framed black-and-white photos. Pretty pricey, though, at $850 per month. It did have a Juliet balcony, so one could at least step outside and taste the air, but the available bedroom was tiny and so narrow as to feel coffin-like. Hal seemed like a decent sort, but he was an actor, which meant he didn't have regular hours outside the home. It also meant that he wanted the whole world to love him, and only felt truly real when he was the centre of attention, preferably with a camera pointed at his professionally whitened teeth. He would always be "on," which could be annoying and emotionally exhausting. His grooming sessions in the bathroom would run long, and he'd probably want to host an annual Oscar party in what I would quickly come to consider *my* living room.

Finally, there was Amy, a university student in a mid-century high-rise just west of Yonge between St. Clair and Davisville. The area was a bit yuppie for my liking, and dull, but the space itself was good—a twelfth-floor penthouse apartment with an open and airy living room/dining room and two large bedrooms, either of which could easily accommodate a king-size bed, dresser and desk. The kitchen was substandard, an absurdly narrow galley affair that would not have looked out of place on a U-boat, but at least the midget-size fridge and stove were relatively new. The most astonishing feature of the apartment was its private rooftop patio, not attached to Amy's corner suite but adjacent to it and accessible through a door in the building's stairwell at the top landing. The thing was colossal. It ran the depth of the building and was at least thirty feet across. It could have easily served as the outdoor space for the entire population of the high-rise, but for some reason it belonged to Amy's apartment alone, even though she already had a regular balcony off her living room. There was a tiny window next to the locked steel entrance door to the roof, just big enough for the rest of the saps in the building to press their noses against and see what they were missing. This exclusive enclave appealed to me enormously, and I had visions of reclining in the sun on one of Amy's blue-and-white-striped cushioned lounge chairs, while she, bikini-clad and straw-hatted, barbecued our dinner and, as the lamb burgers were cooking, refreshed my gin and tonics or applied coconut-scented sunscreen to the less hirsute portions of my dorsal vertebrae.

Amy was a good-looking girl. Not my type, but objectively attractive. I like soft, round, dark-haired women with some thigh and ass. Brown eyes and olive flesh, if we're talking made-to-order. Amy was tall and bony and blue-eyed. She had close-cropped orange hair and the palest skin I'd ever seen. Her cheeks were perpetually flushed, and the effect of the pink on the white of her skin with those blue eyes and the orange hair was startling. She looked like a Victorian doll that had got its hair chopped off by the owner's naughty brother. I didn't want to fuck her, but I wanted to keep looking at her. I wanted to photograph her.

In many ways it seemed like a no-brainer to opt for Amy as a roommate over Vickie or Hal, but one thing that gave me pause was how enthusiastically she was pushing the apartment. She seemed just a little too anxious to have me move in, which made me suspicious. The rent was already very reasonable—$640 per month—and when I asked about cable and phone expenses, she volunteered to take care of the costs, provided I didn't make any long-distance calls that weren't covered by her plan. She didn't appear to mind that I could give her only first month's rent, or that I didn't have an actual employer. And while I didn't know her from a hole in a squirrel's ass, and had no behaviour to compare it to, I sensed that she was behaving unusually nervous and giggly. I'm no beast, but I'm not enough of a stud to provoke blushes and stammers from women. There was something off about it. I told her I'd get back to her.

As I was leaving her apartment, the guy who lived across the hall was leaving his. A sweet hashish smell wafted toward me. The dude was tall, at least six foot three, with shoulder-length locks. The only sign he wasn't in his twenties was the hairline, ebbing a bit on the deeply tanned forehead. He was shirtless and had a faded kaffiyeh draped around his neck. He was wearing sweatpants, Birkenstock sandals and pink, Janis Joplin–style sunglasses. He was actually leaving his home dressed like that. He grinned at me—a stoned-out, Muppety grin—and I sensed in an instant that there could be a lot of gratis grass in my future.

Free pot, free cable, free North American long distance, a private rooftop patio and an easy-to-look-at roommate who would be around too much during the summer, but at school all day in the fall . . . I realized in the elevator as I watched my potential new neighbour put in his earbuds and begin head-bopping to what I recognized as a Nusrat Fateh Ali Khan remix, that I hadn't asked Amy what she was studying. When I got down to the lobby, I buzzed up.

"Hello?"

"Hey Amy, it's John. Sorry to disturb you. It just occurred to me that I forgot to ask about the water pressure."

"Oh. I've never had any problems with it."

"Good. That's good."

"Do you want to come up and check it out?"

"No, no. I trust you. Thanks."

"OK. Just let me know."

"I will. Oh, and Amy, I also forgot to ask what you're studying at school."

A bit of crackle from the intercom, and then: "Does that matter?"

"No. Just curious."

"Psychology" came distorted through the speaker.

"Hmm," I said. "So the pressure's pretty good, huh?"

"It's phenomenal."

"OK, you know what? I think I'm going to go ahead and take the room, if that's all right with you."

"That's great," said Amy.

She buzzed me in.

Truth
What is it?
Where can it be found?
A sculptor knows that the finished piece resides
Fully formed in the unworked stone
The artist's mission is to find and reveal
The Truth within
So it is with us
Let us chip away the years of pain
That obscure and conceal
Let us work away the layers of
Personal and societal subterfuge
Let us discover
And reveal
The Beautiful Truth
Inside
You

theanswertoeverything.org

Amy

The next time I saw him was in a gallery on Spadina. I was off for Christmas break and I went to the K-Space Affordable Art sale, looking for nifty gifts. But even the so-called cheap art was out of my price range. I did score some stocking stuffers, though—white matchbooks with interesting bits of text stamped on them, like: *She was laughing on the outside but smiling wanly on the inside.* Fifty cents each. Not bad.

As I was leaving I heard sounds of a party down the corridor at the Wroblewski Gallery. It turned out to be the opening of a group show of electronic installation art, and front and centre was a piece by John Aarons. It was a Rube Goldberg–like contraption that had a box of photographs on one side and a clear glass container of liquid on the other. A robotic pincer picked up one of the photographs and conveyed it along a kind of ski-lift track to the front of the piece, where it was presented to the viewer. The gizmo featured a big black button labelled *SAVE.* If you pushed the button, the photograph moved back along a track and was deposited safely into a velvet-lined box. If you did nothing, the photograph inched along another track, dropped into the liquid—some kind of hydrochloric acid—and dissolved in a sizzle of chemicals.

These were not digital images that could easily be re-created; these were vintage, one-of-a-kind family photos that had been collected from estate sales and Goodwill. Once they were gone, they were gone forever. There was already a murky slime of dissolved humans and memories floating in the glass vessel.

I stood at the machine for a long time, pressing the big black button. Here comes a little boy in flannel pyjamas, playing with his train set in front of the Christmas tree. *Save.* Here comes a smiling young woman in a cloche hat and flapper coat, her hands in a muff. *Save.* Here are two stern-looking babies, twins I think, in matching frocks and bonnets. *Save.* Here comes an extended family, all dressed up and dapper in front of the Horseshoe Falls *circa* 1950-something. *Save.* I had trouble walking away from the device. And I resented it. It was an uncomfortable burden to have power over the fate of all those people. What was even more chilling was the feeling I had in the moment when I hesitated to push the black button. Why didn't I do it? Why did I let the old lady in the babushka and the housedress and the clunky, untied man shoes disappear? Why didn't I save her? And most disturbing of all, why did I feel a tiny fizz of satisfaction when she was dispatched to the acid bath? I moved off then, headed to the refreshment table and got myself a plastic goblet of wine, and then another, steadying my nerves and gathering the guts to find and confront him. I rehearsed the clever comments I would make about his installation, and the playful conversation that would follow.

I love your piece. And also hate it.

(Laughs.) *Thank you, I think.*

I mean it in a good way. I love that it's truly interactive, that it involves you on more than just a superficial button-pushing level. I just hate that it made me culpable.

Well, that's the point.

It reminds me a bit of what Cronenberg achieved with A History of Violence, *how he made the audience complicit with their blood-lust and desire for revenge.*

I never saw that.

Really? You should try to find it on iTunes or Netflix.

Maybe we could watch it together sometime?

By the time I had played out the scenario to my satisfaction, I had downed four cups of wine and was feeling both tipsy and jumpy. I scanned the room. There he was in the corner, talking to a woman with long, blown-out locks and big boobs. There was something crocodile in his smile. The woman was pressed against the wall, and he was leaning toward her, obviously hitting on her. I waited for a while—a fifth cup of wine—but eventually realized they weren't going anywhere any time soon, and when they did, it would be together.

As I left the gallery, I made straight and fast for the exit. I didn't want to have to glance again at any humans who needed to be saved.

Eldrich

Have you ever had to walk anywhere with a toddler by your side? Maybe a stroll to the corner store or the mailbox or the park? If so, you'll know that it takes three or four times as long to reach your destination. Why? Because children haven't lost the sense of wonder and curiosity that all of us are born with but most of us forsake as we get older.

Children don't move purposefully from point A to point B. They meander. They notice. Here is a dandelion that needs to be sniffed, pulled apart, examined. Here is an ant: a tiny miracle moving along the sidewalk. Here is a wheelchair ramp; I am going to run up and down it just to see what that feels like. Pebbles on a driveway? Let me touch them. Let me feel them crunch under my shoes. Let me throw some. Children are naturally curious and not in a hurry. The journey is more important than arriving at the destination.

It is possible to recapture that sense of inquisitiveness and wonder. Why rush purposefully, with blinkers on, toward death? The world invites us to look around, to take our time, to explore. Let us roam and ramble. Let us question and delve. Let us learn from our former, better selves and embark on what I like to call The Toddler Walk through Life.

John

My ex, Julianne, didn't want to be there when I went to pick up my things. She left the spare key, the one I'd been asked to return (and didn't need, since I'd had it copied long before she ever thought about kicking me to the curb) duct-taped to the bottom of the doormat. I was instructed to leave it on the kitchen table when I was done clearing out my possessions, which would be fewer than I expected, as Julianne had opted to keep my Balint Zsako painting as compensation for seven months of missed rental payments. A thorough ransacking of the apartment proved futile (although I did find and help myself to a quarter vial of pot oil secreted between mattress and box spring). The cunning Julianne had conveyed the work off premises. She had also left me a couple of not-so-subtle messages in the kitchen. One, a picture of her co-worker, the asshole Rob Teskey, secured by a corn-cob shaped magnet to the refrigerator. The other, in case the mug shot wasn't enough of a tipoff that she had moved on in a serious enough manner to warrant large-appliance photo placement, was a poem by the idiot Teskey written for Julianne, folded and tucked inside an envelope on the kitchen table, where I was certain to find, unfold and read it.

Bitch.

The ode was spectacularly awful. I copied it out for use in some future artwork, and then amused myself by annotating it before returning it to the envelope.

Her Name Is Julianne [1]
She curls like a cat in bed [2]
Eyes gleaming [3]
Strong yet soft [4]
Ready to pounce [5]
We roll like thunder in the covers [6]
Her mouth on mine
And everywhere
I want it [7]

Like a vagrant, I moved my paltry possessions east from Christie and St. Clair in a Sobeys shopping cart filched from the parking lot the night before. Amy seemed pleased that I wasn't piling a ton of stuff into our shared domicile, yet perturbed that I would be encamped on an air mattress in the

---

1. Actually, Julianne is her middle name. Her real name is Gladys, which suits her better, since it is also the name of her odious mother, who she is rapidly becoming. Take note, Teskey. Gladys Junior will someday sport a replica of Gladys Senior's bulging belly and bubble butt and like Mommy Dearest will begin to resemble in posture Donald Duck, particularly when waddling to the fridge for another tumbler of Chardonnay.

2. You'll notice, Teskey, that she sounds like one too, should you ever successfully bring her to orgasm, which is doubtful.

3. Orbs alight? What did you do, hold up a handful of cash?

4. Just like bathroom tissue.

5. Someone must have carried a Bundt cake into the bedroom.

6. Elton John called; he wants his line back.

7. Don't get used to it, Teskey; she only goes down for the first couple of months.

large second bedroom. I assured her I was there to stay and would be purchasing a proper bed forthwith. That was a lie. Even a single futon would have set me back a hundred and fifty bucks. All of my funds, the approximately two thousand dollars remaining from a five-thousand-dollar Arts Council grant that had been spent on a photo-dissolving installation piece, were earmarked for rent and my next art project, whatever that happened to be. Also, I had caught a glimpse of Amy's bed during the apartment tour—she wanted to show me how well a king-size fit in the space—and thought it looked mighty comfy. And something about the thought of the moron Teskey getting his dick nibbled by Julianne made it doubly inviting. My plan was to fuck Amy as soon as possible. I had no doubt I could do it, so to make it interesting I set myself a deadline of three weeks in which to slide my way under that wide expanse of Ikea duvet.

Amy

Oddly enough, the next time I saw John Aarons was when he showed up at my door and asked to move in with me.

I had been sharing an apartment with my friend Barb van Vleck, who I'd known since middle school. We got along well and had agreed to stay put until we both graduated and secured jobs—Barb was studying to be an accountant. Then one day out of the blue she told me she had bought herself a condo in the Distillery District and gave me two months' notice. I was pissed off. Not just because I instantly had to find someone reasonable to share my crappy home, or because we had just recently signed on for another shitty year at 55 Hawton Boulevard, but also because Barb and I had talked repeatedly about purchasing a duplex together when we finally had careers and incomes. I would never be able to buy a home on my own in Toronto. Even a 395-square-foot condo like Barb's would be out of reach for the foreseeable future.

When I graduated from high school, my parents gave me money to take the summer off to travel. My mother's people are from Ireland, and my dad's are from Scotland. My folks seemed pleased with the idea of me tramping through the homelands before settling down to my studies. They weren't nearly as pleased when I met Olivio, a thirty-three-year-old Italian, in Dublin and went to live with him in Greece for a year and a half—until he decided to reunite with his ugly wife in Torino. I knew they had been planning to pay for my tuition, but by the time I got home they had changed their Presbyterian minds: "You're an *independent* young woman now, Amy. You'll have to make your own arrangements." I qualified for a couple of small bursaries and worked as a waitress at Kalendar for six months before school started, but mostly I OSAPed myself into a whack of debt. I was jealous of Barb van Vleck, who was almost three years younger than me and already owned her own place. A minuscule place, but cute as hell—exposed brick wall, bamboo floors, poured concrete countertops. And she had what I coveted more than anything in the whole world: her very own washer and dryer. No more contending with the filthy cretins of the building, no more strangers' fecal matter remnants contaminating the underthings. Not for Barb, anyway.

After returning from her luxe condo-warming soirée, my belly sloshing with red wine and resentment, I lay on the floor and made a mental list of some of the things Barb would no longer have to deal with now that she had her own place:

1. **Broken elevators.** There wasn't a single week that I lived at 55 Hawton in which one of the two elevators hadn't been on the fritz. Quite often it was both of them—usually when I got home from a long day at school with a packed knapsack and several bags of groceries, and a head cold and period cramps. That's generally when I had to hoof it up twelve flights of stairs. Oh, and whenever it was horrendously hot and humid outside.

2. **Fire alarms in middle of the night.** In their boundless stupidity, the owners of the building had placed the lobby's pull-down fire alarm three inches above the button that unlocks the inner door and allows residents to exit. Guess what? At 3 a.m., drunk and stoned subnormals were unable to resist pulling the fire alarm on their way out. It happened once or twice a week. Never in my life have I heard a more piercing blast than the air-raid sirens that bansheed me awake on a regular basis. Eventually the fire trucks would arrive. Bleary inhabitants would peer down from balconies, wondering if maybe, maybe this time it was for real. But it never was. Just another night of interrupted rest.

3. **Laundry room hell.** The absolute worst part about living at 55 Hawton: the communal laundry room. It was in the basement in a low-ceilinged, badly lit bunker of a room, a place in which only a rat or a serial killer would want to spend more than thirty seconds. There were five washing machines and five dryers for the entire building. At least one was always out of service. They had never been cleaned. In the middle of the room was what some might generously refer to as a folding table, although I can't imagine anyone letting their clean clothes near this grimy, paint-peeling abomination. If you were not in the laundry room the second your washer or dryer had come to a stop, some degenerate scumbag who had just been scratching his ass or scooping pus out of an open sore would grab your freshly laundered underthings and place them in a heap on this sticky former picnic table. You'd then have to start the process all over again—that is, if you

were lucky enough to find an empty machine, or one without something crazy inside. For some reason the residents of 55 Hawton felt it was acceptable to jam absolutely anything into a washing machine. Some of the items I'd seen put through the wash there: a brown polyester three-piece suit, a pair of ski boots, sofa pillows, automobile floor mats and a fur coat. Not the kind of stuff you want to find when you're about to put your panties in for a spin.

No wonder Barb van Vleck took a powder.

To be honest, I remained bitter and dejected until the day John Aarons showed up at my door. Then I knew it was fate, that Barb's leaving me in the lurch was meant to be. Obviously there was a reason why our paths kept crossing. John Aarons and I were destined to come together. At the time I thought it was for romance. I didn't realize that the powers had a different purpose in mind.

The Universe is Mysterious
And vast
Our joy lies in deciphering its
Inscrutable heart
But can a man born blind know blue?
Are we equipped with the faculty
To crack the code?
Is it enough to open our eyes
If they haven't the capacity to see?
Perhaps if we open our hearts and minds
And the very centre of our souls
The veil will lift
And we will know the rapture
Of gazing upon
The Truth

theanswertoeverything.org

John

Almost all of my known relatives have been murdered. Deliberately starved or gleefully butchered. My mother's people got it from the Young Turks in World War I. The Special Organization. My father's side was nearly erased by the Arrow Cross Party in World War II. The Final Solution.

My parents found each other in a snowstorm in Canada when they passed on a Winnipeg street. She smiled. He fell (figuratively and also in the icy-sidewalk-meeting-your-tailbone sense). Later he would claim he knew in an instant she would become his wife. They had a lot in common. Not gardening or tennis or a taste for classical music. Trauma was their bond. Trumped only by their worship of me. I was the thing that was not supposed to happen. The beating Armenian/Jewish heart in the twenty-first century. The beautiful boy surrounded by millions of absences.

It was late in their lives when I arrived. My father had just turned fifty. My mother was forty-two and subsequently unable to produce more offspring. And so I was the most precious and prized, the treasure that needed to be protected and prepared. The stories they told were not the usual beddy-bye tales. No *Fox in Sox* for me. No *Wind in the Willows*. They told me about corpses stacked like cordwood. They told me about infants tossed into the Black Sea. They told me about showers that weren't really showers, so don't be fooled, my love. Most of the world hates you, they assured me, and would prefer if you didn't exist. Know that and be ready. At the end of the day, your neighbours will not save you. Prayers will not save you. Only you can save you.

Needless to say, I was raised an atheist. There were boxes of matzo in April, but no Seder. There was a Christmas tree in December, but no midnight Mass.

In our house there was no room for God. Not with all the genocide.

Eldrich

Sometimes when things don't go our way, we get frustrated and mad. Sometimes when things are going really badly, we might even get mad at God.

God will not punish you for your anger.

It is your anger that will punish you.

Amy

John Aarons was a mooch and a liar. He paid his first month's rent and then proceeded to sponge off me.

He moved in with nothing but an air mattress, a laptop, some camera equipment and his clothes. Oh, and a single kitchen item: a French press coffee maker. That was it. No furniture. No stereo. No books. He showed up like a homeless person with his entire life heaped in a shopping cart, one that he claimed to have found on the street, but I'm sure he stole from the Sobeys parking lot. He also pretended to return it, but I saw it a few days later, parked next to the Dumpsters beside the high-rises on Lascelles Boulevard—it was missing a couple of wheels at that point, but I'm willing to bet it was the same one. He didn't even bring any bathroom products except for a stone-aged toothbrush and a jumbo bar of Irish Spring, the latter of which was placed on the upper built-in soap dish in the shower but never used. That bar never got any smaller, never even lost its Irish Spring logo imprint, although it grew less distinct over time because of the humidity. Obviously, he was using my pricey oatmeal soap from the health food store. He also helped himself to my very expensive Bumble and Bumble seaweed shampoo. I could smell it halfway across the apartment when he came out of the shower—strutting, of course, in the tiniest of towels—but he denied it. Not that I ever confronted him directly, mind you. I was too smitten. I think I said something lame like "I can get a bigger shower caddy if you want to put some shampoo and stuff in there."

He gave me his wise-ass smirk, knowing exactly what I was getting at. "That's really nice of you," he said. "But don't worry about it. I'm just going to use bar soap on my hair until I start making some cash."

Yeah right. Bar soap. What a joke. His big credo at the time was that as long as he was subsisting on a grant from the Arts Council, he felt a duty to the hard-working taxpayers of the land to live as frugally as possible. Very admirable, I thought. So noble. But considering he was eating my food, drinking my beer, watching my cable, calling Brooklyn and Los Angeles from my phone, and slathering his curls with my premium hair products, who should the hard-working taxpayers of the land have been thanking?

Of course, it was because of John Aarons that I became rich enough to fill a swimming pool with Bumble and Bumble seaweed shampoo, but that's beside the point.

John

In the beginning, Amy turned out to be an even better room-mate than I expected. She was neat and clean and pleasant to be around. And she wasn't around that much. She spent a good deal of time outside the apartment, and a respectable number of hours in her room with the door closed. When she watched TV it was good TV—*Curb Your Enthusiasm; Louie; The Daily Show.* Except for her abominable *Property Brothers* or *Love It or List It* lapses, she was reasonably discerning. She cooked deli-cious food and often shared it with me. Her braised short ribs were divine. Her tortilla soup, superb. She understood that I was an impecunious artist and didn't seem to mind if I used a squirt of her dishwashing liquid or a capful of her laundry detergent. In the early days, anyway, when our love was, ahem, new.

The building, on the other hand, didn't measure up to my expectations. The elevators were maddeningly sluggish, and one or the other seemed to be always out of service. And every few days some sadistic prick would set off the fire alarm in the mid-dle of the night. I do not like to be roused from slumber. It makes me cranky. The only upside was getting to see Amy charge from her bedroom in her typical sleeping attire: tank top and a pair of men's-style cotton briefs. It was pretty. It was very pretty.

The first time we slept together was during one of those fire alarms. It was the third or fourth we'd had since I'd moved in. I was starting to get used to it. The noise would pierce my head like a knitting needle hammered in the ear. I'd lurch into a pair of gotchies and stumble hazy and adrenalized into the living room, at which point Amy, cursing like a knife-stuck sailor, would storm semi-clad from her bedroom. She'd hurtle out the front door, sniff the hallways and stairwells for smoke, then return, muttering and ranting. I'd follow her out onto the living-room balcony (where the cacophony was marginally less of an assault), and we'd look down upon the other balcony people, and the sprinkling of residents in their pyjamas and robes who had actually left the building—generally those with children—and they'd look up at us while we all waited for the fire trucks to arrive and make the horrible noise stop.

On that particular night, I told Amy, "I know why this keeps happening and who's responsible."

"Oh really," she said, giving me a wry but flirty smile. There was a rising tide of flirtation in those early days. The levees were getting ready to burst.

"It's a man who lives in that building across the way. He sneaks over here, pulls the alarm, then runs home and waits for you to come out in your skivvies."

Amy laughed.

"He's watching you right now."

"Yeah, right. So in this day of Internet porn, where you can not only get wide-open beavs at the click of a mouse but virtually any smutty fantasy on earth, including plushy mascots doing it with dwarves—"

"Really? That's out there?"

"Don't pretend you don't know," said Amy.

"OK. Busted. It's my homepage."

"Uh-huh. Right. So highly unlikely that buddy over there is going to leave his home and go to all that trouble just to see a skinny chick in her underwear."

"Not just any skinny chick," I said, inching closer.

Sirens could be heard in the distance as Amy and I, still looking down upon the scene, slid toward each other along the balcony railing, pressing first our arms together, then our heads and finally—as the fire trucks screamed into view—our lips. Very rom-com except for the nauseating racket.

It was a strange sensation having sex with Amy. She was so much bonier than any woman I'd ever been with. Usually I am aware only of the pressure of flesh. Now there seemed to be rib cage and elbow and kneecap involved. It was different. But I liked it. I liked it a lot, not least because of Amy's incredible responsiveness—a rousing thing to behold.

The alarm ended almost immediately after we did, which, in our giddy state, caused much hilarity. We got up, ate cold chicken and Fudgeos, and then fucked again. After, she tickled my back. I remember that very clearly. It was the first time she did it—trailing her long cold fingers up and around my spine. It felt sublime and struck me as more intimate than anything Julianne had done in the three years we had been together. I conked while she was at it, just before dawn. I woke up at noon, alone under Amy's floral duvet, which smelled faintly and pleasantly of lemons.

It was three weeks to the day after I'd moved in.

Eldrich

There are only two mistakes you can make on the road to Truth. Not going all the way, and not starting.

John Aarons was my friend. Together we embarked upon the road to Truth, but John did not go all the way. His passion became misdirected. He let Shakespeare's green-eyed monster into his heart, and in this darkness he lost his way.

John Aarons left the Institute in January 2013.

John Aarons is not to blame.

Amy

I think he got the idea early on.

In the first weeks that we lived together, and even after we slept together, I guess a couple of months after he moved in, John was hanging out more with Eldrich than he was with me. I thought it was bizarre. I mean, back then I had pegged Eldrich as some pot-addled mental deficient who happened to live across the hall. I would see him all the time around the building and also in the park, where he played his weirdo instruments, but we weren't friendly. In fact, the only time I ever spoke to him was when I was kicking him off my private rooftop terrace, accessible, unfortunately, from the stairwell beside my apartment and not directly from inside my apartment. I would ask him to leave and please never return. He would grin and agree, and then two days later I'd find him out there again. I didn't even get angry because I thought he was retarded. I really did. I figured head injury or something. He had that slow, ponderous way of speaking, and that perpetual almost-smile that made him look like a tipsy golden retriever. The way he dressed was ridiculous, everything mismatched and tattered, and his mother—I assumed it was his mother—came around every few days with CorningWare casseroles or plates of food covered in foil. I figured he was a simp, beating his congas for spare change in the park and surviving on some kind of government disability fund while Mommy kept him fed and very occasionally bathed.

I couldn't have been more wrong. And the fact that he continued to appear on my terrace, even though I'd had the locks changed on the giant steel entrance door, should have been my first clue.

John

It didn't take long to insinuate myself into the ambit of Eldrich. I expected to encounter him mainly in the building, but our first real exchange occurred out of doors about a week and a half after I'd moved in. To get from our apartment to the better stores and subway you had to first pass through a park. A winding concrete walkway bisected it. On one side was a playground bubbling with toddlers and their Filipino nannies, a non-functioning splash pad and two weedy tennis courts. The other side was just grass and trees and benches on which lovers lolled and derelicts loafed. This is where Eldrich set up shop, so to speak, on a bench beside a prodigious willow in the crook of the path.

Eldrich, I discovered, was a busker. He played (I use the term casually, as none of his musical meanderings were evidently melodious) a variety of instruments, all of them unusual. He slapped happy on a Peruvian box drum, hammered a Chinese dulcimer with bamboo sticks, and bowed something called a nyckelharpa that looked like a violin with a set of wooden keys grafted onto it. But the strangest contraption, and the one I liked best, was a tripod with a chunk of wood at the top, and a thin, flat wooden tongue clamped horizontally atop that. There was a long overhang (think of a ruler held over the edge of a desk), and the tongue was made to vibrate by striking or bowing it. A wedge of fretted wood pressed against it controlled the pitch. The wooden tongue was interchangeable for different sounds, and these objects were very beautiful—smoothed into curvy shapes that reminded me of faux-African sculptures from a 1950s rec room. The thing sounded like nothing I'd heard before. It was unearthly, kooky, like the background music to a crazed parade of Dr. Seuss characters, and it provided the perfect opening to conversation in the park on a sunny day.

"Wow. That's nutty. What is that thing?"

"It's a daxophone."

"*Dax*ophone?"

"Yup. Wanna try it?"

As I was coaxing out a few *galunks* and *gazoings*, two extraordinarily braless hippie chicks bounced over and presented Eldrich with a Tim Hortons iced cappuccino, an apparently homemade sandwich wrapped in paper towel, and an envelope, which he quickly stuffed into the side pocket of his cargo shorts.

"Mindy, Alexa, this is my neighbour from across the hall . . . ?"

"John," I said, a little surprised that Eldrich knew I had moved in, given that I had passed him only once in the lobby since I'd lived there, and he hadn't acknowledged me at all.

"Hi," said Mindy and Alexa, glancing quickly at me and then turning their eyes and nipples back toward Eldrich, who was transferring busker coins from his daxophone case into a leather pouch.

"Anyone want to smoke a joint?" he said.

Ten minutes later I was seated on an orange vinyl sofa (very mod except for the duct-taped cracks), gobbling half an avocado, red pepper and alfalfa sprout sandwich on pumpernickel. Delicious. Healthy too. Eldrich was busy rolling up the contents of the mystery envelope, while Mindy and Alexa assaulted us with an insipid story about being on all-night bear patrol during a tree-planting excursion in the wilds of British Columbia. I smiled at the ostensibly amusing parts, and kept myself awake by sneaking peeks at their chests and other overexposed, predictably tattooed parts. Alexa had the superior rack, but she also had white-girl dreadlocks—inexcusable, if you ask me. Mindy had regular, conceivably shampooed hair but sported a dirty nose ring, which I had to not look at or think about while I was eating. I decided that I wouldn't sleep with either of them and turned my attention to a hangnail that required a delicate chewing away.

"The bear was pissed off 'cause Roman and Daryl had laughed at him earlier in the day," said Mindy, explaining why a feral animal in the middle of the wilderness had bitten through a tree planter's presumably food-containing tent.

Her idiot confederate nodded vigorously. "It's true!" she said, giggling.

I remained unconvinced but smiled mildly as Mindy launched into another tedious tale, this one about her travels in Thailand. As she jawed, I noted that Eldrich's apartment was the mirror opposite of Amy's minus my bedroom. He had the same parquet flooring (vestibule four squares by six squares), the same galley kitchen with shrimp-o appliances, the same pink toilet, sink and tub dating from 1950-something in the bathroom. Things were set up differently, though. Instead of having a dining table in the small nook outside the kitchen, he had placed his table and chairs by the living-room window, the natural place for a sofa. His dining-room nook was filled with musical instruments, and his couch had been plonked nonsensically in the middle of the living room on a diagonal. There was no coffee table, and only one chair—a wicker thing, *circa* 1972, with a giant rounded back that had a peacock-tail design woven through it. Between the couch and chair was an ottoman strewn with ugly-covered small-press poetry books and a muffin tin that served as an ashtray (or twelve little Siamese ashtrays). There was a milk-carton shelving unit against one wall, holding books, a stereo and CDs. The world's largest didgeridoo leaned against the opposite wall. There were a lot of outrageously healthy-looking house plants and many candles in all shapes and sizes. No TV though. No TV in the bedroom either—I peeked on my way back from taking a piss.

"Should we smoke these on the roof?" Eldrich held up two skilfully prepared spliffs.

"Sure," said Mindy.

"Cool," said Alexa.

Amy hadn't yet made me my own key for the patio, and I told Eldrich as much.

"No problem," he said, grinning and straightening. "C'mon." He grabbed an empty milk crate from the side of the Sealtest bookcase and we followed him into the stairwell leading to the outdoor space. Eldrich slid open the tiny window next to the locked steel door, placed the milk carton on the floor and stood on it. He poked one arm and his head through the opening and then, with a sharp shrug, proceeded to dislocate his left shoulder before slithering through like a snake.

"Ew," squealed Mindy. "Freaky."

"Awesome," breathed Alexa.

Eldrich let us onto the patio, retrieved the milk carton, closed and relocked the door.

"Doesn't that hurt?" I asked as I stretched out on one of Amy's two padded lounge chairs. Oddly, no one chose to make use of the other. Eldrich parked himself on the overturned milk carton. Alexa and Mindy sat cross-legged on the ground beside him.

"Pain is inevitable; suffering's optional," said Eldrich on the inhale, smiling through smoke as he sparked both joints and handed one to each bobble-headed maiden at his feet.

Is that so? I had the urge to pop him one hard in the nose, knock him off his perch. But I had a presentiment that he'd merely right himself, wipe away the blood and cartilage and keep smiling his maddeningly vague, I-know-something-you-don't-know smile.

Eldrich

Conquer the angry man by love. Conquer the ill-natured man by goodness. Conquer the miser with generosity. Conquer the liar with truth.

People say things. They say a lot of things. Mouths open and close. Things dribble and fly out. But this is the truth. What I was doing before John and Amy came along was exactly what I was doing after John and Amy, and the same thing I've been doing my whole life: making music (or more accurately *finding* and *channelling* music), thinking about the best way to live every moment I've been granted here on earth, connecting with God in as many ways as possible, sharing what I've learned with my friends and allowing my friends to share with me.

I never tried to organize anything. Ever. John and Amy did all that.

Friends
And family
Sometimes
Let you down
Sometimes
Sadness eclipses all
You need
Something
You need
Relief
Peace
Forgiveness
Comfort
You need
To find me
Now

theanswertoeverything.org

John

After many barren moons, I finally sprouted an idea for my next art project. MAMA. I would construct a humongous mother with a walk-in womb. She would be giant and reclining, big enough to make a large man feel like an infant. She would be built out of lightweight materials, perhaps papier-mâché. Or maybe wire and a not-quite-opaque skin, illuminated from within to give her a slight glow. Her hair would flow out across the floor. Her breasts would swell and hang, and the nipples would protrude rudely. In her pelvis would be an opening, a secret door to a cozy cavity. The viewer would enter and tuck themselves inside. A fetal shape to ensure the correct cashew curl of body. Total darkness with the door shut. And softness all around. Sponge? Chinchilla? Warmth, of course. And a speaker with the gurgle and rush of fluids. A sloshy heartbeat. Also, the suggestion of voice through liquid. I would find an audio whiz to get it right. MAMA's murmurs would be unrecognizable through the murk, but she'd be saying: *I love you, baby . . . Mama loves you sooo much.* There'd be a timer to secretly record and chart how long each individual stayed inside.

I was excited by the idea. And also daunted. I would have

to rent a huge studio space in which to build and display my creation. She would be tricky to assemble. A technician would have to design a proper ventilation system for the womb.

It was going to take a lot of moolah to make MAMA.

Amy

So, of course, I started hearing about Eldrich from John, who seemed to be growing increasingly fascinated with what I thought was our brain-dead neighbour. *He's not as daft as he looks, you know* was the line I heard in the early days. Then: *I think he's actually got it figured out more than most people.* And regularly: *I mean, the guy has never had a job in his life.* That was the part John was most impressed with, the fact that Eldrich had made it well into adulthood and continued to get along quite nicely, thank you, without ever being employed. *Not even a paper route*, he'd say with a mouth full of marvel. *No real jobs ever!* Even John, King Mooch, had a smattering of T4s in his past.

The groupies were what really floored him. John told me that busker Eldrich had people who regularly journeyed to the park to shower him with offerings—food, marijuana, money. One woman would even show up with housewares she'd purchased from garage sales: a never used, still-in-the-box humidifier; an almost complete set of Ikea wineglasses; even one of those über-expensive cast-iron jobbies from Le Creuset that she'd miraculously scooped for ten bucks at a rummage sale. I coveted that thing even though it was stained and the handle was cracked in half. John couldn't believe that anyone would go out of their way to ferry gifts to Eldrich, a man who didn't seem to possess more than an ounce of tuneful talent. But then John realized that the groupies were more interested in Eldrich's musings than in his music. He would busk for a bit during the morning and afternoon rush hours—the park was a conduit from our residential hub to the subway, so lots of people passed through it each day—but mostly he'd just hang out on his bench beside his instrument of choice, blabbing on subjects philosophical or spiritual, and the groupies would gather to listen. *Not just raptly*, John would tell me, *devotedly*. I remember he initially referred to them as "groupies" but soon came to see Eldrich's supporters as something other. There was this one night—it must have been near the beginning of September because I had just started back at school—it was stupidly hot and humid, but we'd had sex anyway. John had barely slid his sweaty self off me when I saw the gears in his brain lurch into action and start whirring. His toes were all tap and twitch at the end of the bed, and he couldn't even wait a respectful twenty seconds before he was on about his favourite subject.

"I spent the day with Eldrich in the park again."

"Hmm," I said. "Must be nice." I wasn't really enjoying being back at school. I was thinking maybe I had made a mistake about what to study, and that maybe I should have gone into something practical—business admin, or even accounting, like Barb van Vleck.

"Well, I had to endure a certain amount of balalaika and blah blah blah, but it was worth it to get a read on things."

"What do you mean?"

"He has more followers than I thought. And not just the types you'd expect."

"Hmm." I watched him peel the condom off and inspect it. He always did that. He seemed to be measuring the volume of semen, but maybe he was checking for leaks.

"Yesterday, this guy shows up at around three. Asian. Expensively dressed, Fendi sunglasses, killer watch . . ."

"Yeah."

"I've never seen a watch like this in my life. Tiny dude. Reminded me of Ren from *Ren & Stimpy*. Remember that?"

"Yeah."

"Unhealthy looking. Apparently, he used to own one of those big-ass monster homes that back onto the park. Used to go for walks out there and started having confabs with Eldrich."

"Hmm."

"Here's the bizarre thing. The guy moved. He bought a mansion up around the Bridle Path, but he still comes to the park to talk to Eldrich."

"That's weird."

"I know. The guy's like fifty-something and stinking rich. I'm guessing some kind of corporate thief who could afford all manner of shrinks and what have you, but he drives to Oriole Park to talk to Eldrich. He was there yesterday. And he stopped by today too."

"What do they talk about?"

"Yesterday it was New Agey stuff. Buddy had read some book Eldrich recommended and he was all excited about it. Today he shows up and they wander off for a private conversation. They didn't talk long. I saw him slip Eldrich something, which I think was a roll of cash. And it looked pretty thick. Then five-foot-two buddy gives six-foot-something Eldrich a big hug and takes off. I watched him go back to his car. Some super-snazzy convertible. I think it was foreign."

"Maybe Eldrich is selling him drugs?"

"No. No way. Eldrich doesn't buy drugs. He has these hippie chicks who supply him with smoke for his own personal use. They just give it to him. Just 'cause. He never has more than a few joints worth."

"Hmm."

"You should've seen this guy's watch. It was like a cylinder with the clock face on the side, and on top was a window into the works of the thing. Must have cost a pant-load."

"Hmm."

"And you know that woman you thought was his mom?"

"The one who brings food?"

"Yeah. It's not his mom. It's this lady named Joyanne who cooks for him because she thinks he's the bee's knees. Eldrich says he gives her 'counsel.'"

"Counsel? Wow. I can't imagine taking counsel from a guy who wears Birkenstocks with purple socks."

"Yeah. And she's not alone in her devotion. He's got the hippie maidens and a few mangy park rats who hang around all the time. And there are four or five other people—seemingly unmedicated, employed humans who I met over the last couple of days. Plus Richie Rich with the watch. That's like a dozen of what Eldrich calls his "friends." But these aren't friends, Amy. I wouldn't even call them followers. These people, I believe, are *disciples*."

"Hmm." There was something about the way he was looking at me that made me uncomfortable. As if he expected me to do something. To act.

"I just think there's an opportunity here," he said as I got up and left the room. I went to take a pee, and then grabbed a bottle of Perrier from the kitchen. When I returned he was sitting up against the headboard, biting his nails, cogitating.

"What kind of opportunity?" I said, climbing back into bed.

"I don't know," he said. "I'm an installation artist. You're studying psychology—group dynamics, all that stuff. Maybe we could use Eldrich and his supporters as inspiration. Maybe craft a little . . . experiment slash art piece?"

I laughed. "Do you know how complicated it is to craft a viable psychological study?"

"Not really."

"Well, it's a lot of work, especially if you want to design something that isn't full of flaws and ultimately useless."

"OK."

"It's like any other field of science. You have to use the scientific method."

"I remember that. Sort of."

"You start with an observation. Like, you notice the leaves turn colour in the fall. So you generate a hypothesis to explain it: *I think the leaves turn colour when the temperature drops.*"

"Right."

"Then you come up with a prediction: *If leaves turn colour when the temperature drops, I predict that exposing a tree to low temperatures will cause the leaves to turn colour.*"

"Pretty simple."

"But then you have to design an experiment to test your hypothesis—something that can be replicated to support your findings. In the tree-leaf case, it would be easy, but in the case of anything to do with the psychology of humans, it's never that straightforward."

"But it's doable. They do studies all the time."

"Yeah. But for every study out there, there's a counter-study refuting the findings or poking holes in the methodology. Like this famous study on the misattribution of arousal, which is when you get excited for a specific reason, but you chalk it up to something else. So say I go on a blind date and I order a decaf, but the waiter fucks up and gives me a double shot of espresso. So I'm drinking my coffee, talking to my date, and my heart starts pounding, I feel alert, energized, and I think, 'Wow, I really like this guy.' But it's not the guy, it's the caffeine. I misattribute the sensations."

"That's a real thing?"

"Yeah, it's real. So anyway, they did this study involving bridges. One was a safe sturdy thing, the other was a rickety suspension bridge strung high over a river. I think it was the Capilano Suspension Bridge, actually. Anyway, they put an attractive woman at one end of each bridge and she would ask the males who crossed over some questions, ostensibly some kind of survey, then she'd give them her phone number and tell them they could get in touch if they had any questions. So the hypothesis was that the males on the suspension bridge would misattribute their arousal from crossing the dangerous bridge to an attraction to the interviewer, and that more of them would call her than would those who took the safer route."

"And did they?"

"Yeah. Way more males from the suspension bridge called. But this is what I'm talking about. The study was flawed. It had to be completely redesigned, because males who chose to cross the scary bridge instead of the safe bridge may just have been predisposed to take risks, so more likely to go out on a limb and contact the attractive interviewer anyway."

"Hmm."

"It's not as simple as you think."

"OK."

"And what is it that you want to learn, anyway? I mean, is it really so intriguing that a dozen misfits like to listen to Eldrich's New Age ramblings?"

"I don't know. Maybe not."

He made a joke then, something about slipping caffeine pills into my dinner when he wanted to have his way with me, but I knew he was still thinking about Eldrich, about Opportunity. And I knew exactly what it was that had turbo-charged his interest. It wasn't curiosity about the human mind, or the psychology of religion, or the prevalence of New Age practitioners in an increasingly secular society. No. It was the dude with the cylindrical watch and the snazzy car and the fat roll of cash.

John

Observation: Eldrich has attracted a number of followers who view him as a spiritual guru and go out of their way to provide him with tithes.

Hypothesis: If a dozen or so individuals are prepared to follow Eldrich in this manner, then others will be too.

Prediction: Increasing awareness of Eldrich and his teachings will lead to an increase in the number of Eldrich supporters (and their offerings).

Easy-peasy. Let the experiment begin.

On the Darkest
Night
Of the Coldest
Day
A Radiant Sun
Awaits
You may not see or
Feel it
But it's there
Waiting to Rise and
Light Your Way
Waiting to Rise and
Warm You

theanswertoeverything.org

Amy

I guess the first thing he did was create the website. THEANSWERTOEVERYTHING.ORG. Very understated. Not promising much there. Then he started putting up flyers to lead people to the site. He used fluorescent-orange paper, so the things really popped. I'd see them all over—subway, grocery stores, cafés, bars. He'd be out for hours at a time, taping and stapling to whatever didn't move. Each poster had some kind of warm, fuzzy, Eldrich-type message on it, and then the website address across the bottom: www.theanswertoeverything.org. That was it.

The site, at that point, was simple. Just a splash page with another one of those inspirational messages superimposed over a photo of a sun-dappled body of water. There were three buttons at the bottom, for each of the following interactive responses: *Comment*; *Confess*; *Share*. If you clicked on any of those, you were taken to a blank page on which to type and send. He thought about displaying these posts on a kind of message board so everyone could see and react to them, but I talked him out of it. I figured he'd be spending half his time policing the site and deleting posts, since I expected the majority of responses to come from Douglas Adams fans—*The answer is 42*—or snarky teens who wanted to prank us.

Boy was I wrong.

✉ Heather

I don't know why I'm doing this. I don't do anything anymore, let alone write to strangers. Funny how you can go from someone who does a million things—job, mom, Community Crafters Club, Dragon Boat Festival Committee—to someone who does nothing. Yesterday I went for a walk. It was the first time I've been past the property line since I moved here. I get my groceries delivered. There's a good service for that. And my prescriptions and anything else I need. My sister used to visit every couple of months. But that's ended. I don't care. She has no idea. She thinks she does, but she doesn't. And her visits exhaust me. I don't have the energy for her silence or her sighs. For her bright blouses and her disapproval. Just think-ing of her sitting in the corner with her white pants and her orange pedicure makes me tired. I like it dark and quiet down here. Nobody blazing in the corner, thank you very much. This is the only place I can imagine living now. Underground. Like a mole. I have mushrooms growing between the tile cracks in my shower. The only mushrooms around here. I don't cook anymore. I used to cook every day. I used to make all these sneaky recipes because my baby didn't like vegetables. I had to be clever about it. Hide things inside pasta noodles and cover them with cheese sauce. Roll a broccoli floret in a piece of pepperoni, roll that in cheese, cover it in pizza dough and bake. I was good at it. I made muffins that were full of zucchini, but nobody could tell. Those muffins were a big hit. Now all my food is frozen.

The people upstairs have no idea that I used to be normal. Sometimes I see them in the laundry area or the backyard and I can tell what they're thinking. But I don't care. I couldn't care less what I look like. They are in a different world than I am. I used to be in that world, and I had no idea there was anything outside it. That has been a real eye-opener—to discover that there is a dark underworld going at the same time as the regular sunlit world. Everything was so normal for so long. When I was growing up, I can't think of one un-normal thing that ever happened. There was a girl in my sister's class at Canadore who got paralyzed in a car crash. But that didn't happen to me. And it's pretty normal for a teenager to get into a car accident, especially around North Bay, with all the moose on the highway. They like the salt on the roads. That girl's boyfriend hit a moose on Highway 11. The boyfriend wasn't hurt at all. Some people get paralyzed and some walk away without a scratch.

My husband was super-normal. Paul Bauer. A home inspector. A coach at the summer hockey camp for kids. A large man. Handy. He liked his beer and his sports and his workshop. I liked the way he looked and that he could do everything well. He could rewire a house, build a deck, fix his own truck and drive anywhere and back without looking at a map, let alone one of those GPS devices that he used to scoff at. He never went to the doctor, never got sick. I liked how he would pick me up and carry me around and call me "Feather" instead of Heather. Sometimes strangers would think he was my dad because he was so big and mature-looking; he always looked like a grown-up, even in high school, and I was always such a shrimp and kept looking like a teenager even into my thirties. I liked the grandfather clocks he used to make in the workshop and sell at cost to our friends. He was the best home inspector around. Everyone wanted Paul Bauer. He never missed a thing. He really cared about doing everything correctly. He had integrity. He had a jean jacket that smelled a little like tobacco from the one cigarette he enjoyed in the yard every night after dinner. I loved that smell. Snow and smoke.

Gosh, this is strange. It's making me remember a time before hate. I don't feel it, but I can remember it. I need to sleep now. Maybe I'll finish this later.

✉ Keith

To whom it may concern,

When I was fourteen, I forgot to let the dog back in when I came home for lunch. I let him out but he didn't come back in time, then I had to leave for school and I didn't think about it when I left. I guess I figured he was still inside or I forgot about him being out. I didn't think about it is the point. After school I went down to our spot by the drain, but it was so cold none of my friends were there. Then Dave showed up and said everyone was probably at McDonald's, so we went over and hung around until we got kicked out for not buying enough. When I went home, Harley was at the door, shivering real bad. They said it was minus thirty that day with the wind chill. Harley had snow chunked up all over his face. I took him in and got the snow off and tried to warm him up, but I couldn't get him to quit shaking. I made a bath and thought that was working, but it didn't. After I got him out and dried him off, he passed out. He was still breathing but he was passed right out. Then I couldn't wake him up and a few minutes later he passed away.

It was my fault but I never told no one. When my mom got home from work, I said I found him that way after school. She said he was real old and don't feel bad. But it's hard not to feel bad when your mom is crying all night for a week for her best dog. And when you keep picturing his face so happy to see you, even when he's shivering so bad and not blaming you at all for what you done. Or when you think of him passed away on the bathmat all the time. And you see how small he was with his fur all wet. Even twenty years later you dream about it. Every couple of weeks or so. And practically every time you get out of the shower you can't help thinking about it. And you know God never forgave you for that sin and has pretty much been punishing you with stuff ever since. That's my confession.

✉ Anne-Marie

Hey there,

    I just wanted to say I think your signs are so true and they've been a pleasure to read! I didn't notice the website at first. I just thought someone really neat and thoughtful was sharing some beautiful messages with the world. And so I was really pleased when I finally noticed it on the board at Alternative Grounds. Who are you? Are you around Roncesvalles?

    I don't really have anything in particular to share. I'm just a spiritual person who is looking for guidance and knowledge on the road to illumination. I am interested in finding my spiritual path, no matter what that is or which way it leads. I've been reading a lot about Wicca and paganism, which seem to be very inclusive and gentle. I respect all people's right to believe what they believe, but I'm not into organized religions. I'm interested in Gaia, certain Sufi traditions, holistic health and healing. I love nature, and I'm committed to ecology and living my life without leaving a huge footprint on the world, except in the caring sense! I would love to know more about your organization. You can email me at annemarieknits@yahoo.ca. I have a small knitting business. I sell hand-dyed yarn and knitted goods. I use only organic wool, cotton and hemp, and 100 percent natural dyes, like beet juice, turmeric and rosehips. I would like to steer my son onto the right path with me. He's a teenage boy who is also in need of guidance. Cheers!

✉ Ibrahim

Dear Answer to Everything,

My wife is have trouble conceiving. Can you give advice?
Reply me immediately? iakim57@sympatico.ca

✉ Drew

Hello,

I've been kind of depressed lately. My job sucks and I don't have a girlfriend. I have a club I go to when I can afford it and when they let guys in alone, but it's not the same and it's pretty expensive. It's not working girls at the club, by the way. It's real people who want to get together. It's all controlled and very clean. But it's only once a month that they let men in without a partner. I'm saving up to get a condo and a proper girlfriend, but my job is terrible and the real estate keeps going up and it seems like I'll never get out of this place, which I hate.

I live in a room in a house at Jarvis and Gerrard. I have my own fridge and hotplate, and I bought a small chest freezer to save money on bulk purchases, which was a good idea, since it's already paid for itself twice over. I have to share a bathroom, though. And the people here are pigs. Total depressing pigs. If I didn't clean the sink, it would never get cleaned. Seriously. I did an experiment once to see if anyone else would clean it if I stopped doing it. No. Of course not. I finally broke down and cleaned it after three weeks. I couldn't stomach it anymore. You should see the hair slime I have to pull out of the drain every couple of months. Disgusting. I asked the girls not to comb their hair over the sink, but they still do it, even though they claim they don't. I pull the evidence out of the drain every six weeks, so I know they do it. They won't even flush properly. You have to flush the toilet two or three times sometimes because the plumbing is bad, but they don't wait to do it. They're too selfish to wait for the tank to fill up. It's sickening. Depressing. The worst one isn't even the crazy alky or the working girls. It's the Ryerson student. Griffin something or other. Ironic. The guy who's taking journalism lessons and comes from some upper-class household. The working girls flush more than he does. Not only doesn't he flush properly, he buzz-cuts his hair in there and covers the whole place in tiny black hairs, which he doesn't clean up properly and which end up in my room, stuck to my socks and whatnot. The super doesn't care. He barely speaks English. I have to do the cleaning, and I have neck and shoulder pain, which is getting worse all the time. I'll be so glad when I can get out of this place. Which is who knows when, given the rising real estate market. The more I save, the higher it gets. I can't catch up. I work for Blood Services, at the call centre. I'm not selling anything but people still get peeved when you call them. Plus my employers can't seem to get it straight who to call. Half the time I'm supposed to call someone to tell them about a blood drive because it says they haven't given blood for over a year and they're like, "Piss off, dude, I gave blood last week, get your records straight." So it's depressing. My mom thinks I should move back to Brampton, where I could get a nice condo for a lot less, but I don't want to. For one thing, my mom's there. Ha ha. I love her and all, but she's a plus-size lady and not mobile and

I'd basically be her personal slave if I went back. Also it would be even harder to find a proper girlfriend or job in Brampton. And there are no clubs like the club I occasionally go to. I'd rather not go to the club but sometimes I break down. I love Jesus Christ and I hope your signs are about Him. I think they are. I'd like to come for a meeting sometime. Please let me know if you ever have any. Sometimes I go to the Jarvis Street Baptist Church, because it's close. But I'm not a Baptist. I tried to go to St. Luke's but it's screwed up. It says United on the sign, but there's always a different congregation in there. And usually not English. Filipino or whatnot. I think they just rent it out to different foreigners, which is fine but doesn't work for me. Anyway, let me know if there are any meetings. I've been feeling kind of depressed lately, so it would be good.

✉ Ibrahim

Dear Answer to Everything,

    We are doing all things you say. Thank you. Thank you for putting her predicament to the top of group prayer agenda. You are very kind. I would make a donation. Advise please where to send? iakim57@sympatico.ca

✉ Heather

I guess part of me wants to talk about this, but not to anybody I know. And part of me thinks that seeing your sign the other day was an omen. It was on the post at the end of my street and must have just been taped there, since we had rain all morning. I went out about an hour after the storm and there it was. Perfectly dry. Since it was the first time I'd left the house in over a year, it felt like it had been put there for me. And so I've decided to continue on. Or at least try.

I'll start when things were good, when I got pregnant again and we were so happy. I had been pregnant before, twice before, but it hadn't worked out. Both times I had miscarried in the tenth week or thereabouts, so when we made it to week sixteen that third time, we finally let ourselves get excited again. Paul really wanted a son. And I really wanted a daughter. I guess that was the first sign of trouble, but we didn't know it. We used to joke about it. Paul would talk about all the things he was going to do with his fine boy—make a rink out back for hockey, go snowmobiling on the trails, build stuff in the workshop. And I'd sass back with all the things I was going to do with my sweet girl—make a playhouse in the yard and decorate it, have tea parties with homemade squares and cakes, design clothes for her Barbies. I used to sew quite a bit. I made all the drapes in our house, and lots of pretty doll clothes for my nieces. Paul was sure we were going to have a boy. He wanted to paint the nursery blue, but I wouldn't let him. He said blue was good for a girl too. But I said no, we were keeping it white until the baby was born because I wanted pink if it was a girl. Then the five-month ultrasound was coming up. We agreed that we still didn't want to know and asked the technician not to tell us. But after, Paul was acting all cocky and smug. He wouldn't stop smiling. And he played the drums on the steering wheel all the way home, I remember that, the sound of his wedding ring tapping the wheel and him singing to the radio, which he never did. It was that song "Good Day Sunshine."

At first he wouldn't tell me why he was acting strange. But that night in bed he apologized and said he accidentally looked at the ultrasound screen and saw we were having a boy. He said he saw his "thing." I didn't believe him. Even if he thought he was right, I didn't think he could tell. I had also peeked at the ultrasound screen, and all I could see was hazy grey shapes. You could hardly even tell it was a baby, let alone a girl or boy. I thought it was impossible to tell with just one look. And it bugged me that the very next day he painted the nursery blue even though I asked him to please wait. And that's when I made the second biggest mistake of my life. That's when I got all prideful and went against my husband and nature. That's when I went into the nursery after Paul was asleep and got down on my knees beside the little pine cradle and prayed with all my heart for God to please, please give me a girl.

My first big failure.

My second biggest mistake.

I'm sorry. This is much more difficult than I thought it was going to be.

✉ Tyson

Atheism = Satanism. Jesus battled Satan in the desert and we are battling Satan in the streets, in the schools, in our homes and hearts. Repentance, faith and obedience can save us. We must not fall from felicity to misery. Prayer is what we need to stand firm. Make no mistake. This is a war. This is a war with the great deceiver, the insidious schemer who will leave no soul untempted. I recognize the fullness of God in your posts. I would like to join you in spiritual warfare against the beast and his malicious and devious devices. Tell me where and when and I'll be there with the armour of God's love and the sword of faith held high.

✉ Catelyn

Your posters are so great. Thanks!!! I'm a single mom and it's hard right now. I have some savings from working at Shield Assurance Company and things were going good, but then I slipped up with an ongoing situation and got let go. I'm back on track now, but they won't hire me back and I can't look for new jobs with my daughter to take care of. I can't just leave her with anyone, because we all know how that goes.

My ex's mom was supposed to take care of Staci when I went back to work, but then she had to get a job because her boyfriend split to go work with his brothers on an oil rig. Staci's dad doesn't pay support because he's unemployed. I don't think he's trying so hard to get a job. He's a drummer and wants to start a new band. He says he's going to get famous and rich and buy a house for Staci and me to live in. That would be nice, but I'm not holding my breath. I support his dream and all, I just wish he would take a part-time job to help out. His mom watches Staci sometimes and makes dinners when we go over, but she can't help with support. Todd says he can't watch Staci during the day because he has to practise and look for work. It's true that he's practising, but I don't think he's looking. I told him he could probably get a training position at Shield

Assurance to do what I was doing, underwriting assistant, but he says he'd rather kill himself than work in the insurance industry, which isn't very nice considering that was my career. I've been paying for everything for the last three years and I didn't hear him disrespecting the insurance industry then, if you know what I mean.

Anyway, your posters are a wind beneath my wings whenever I see them. I do feel like I'm struggling. And it's hard to stay positive. I have had troubles with substance abuse, but I'm trying to stay clean for my daughter's sake. I'm good now. But it's rough. I go to meetings but half the time the meetings make it worse if this guy is there. There's this old guy in group who is always going off about all the bad stuff in the world, like talking about how all the food we eat is genetically modified and the companies don't care if we get cancer so long as they can make more money and put the real farmers out of business. And about how all the bees are dying from pesticides, so there won't be any food in the future anyways, and forget fish because the oceans are full of oil spills and the chemicals to get rid of it and nuclear waste from Japan, which is making all the fish toxic and all the shrimp deformed in the Gulf of Mexico. He said there's a garbage dump of plastic water bottles swirling around in the middle of the ocean that's bigger than an entire nation. I don't know if I believe that one. I mean, why would they end up all together in one spot? And then yesterday he was saying how the USA is releasing killer viruses in China to test them as weapons, like a special bird flu that will end up here because even Chinese from remote villages fly to Toronto quite often. And he was going on about antibiotics that don't work anymore and how, if you go to the hospital just to get stitches, you'll end up dying from germs they can't cure that are starting to spread into gyms and the subway, on the poles and such. Then he said it won't matter anyhow since the Arctic ice is melting and underneath is the same poison gas that killed the dinosaurs, and all the humans are going to die out much sooner than scientists thought. So it's really messed up and scary and really hard to stay positive. But you have to stay positive for your kids, right? I have to be hopeful for the future and for my daughter. And your messages are helping me stay hopeful. They're like a whole other side to the story. So thanks!!!! :)

✉ Wayne

I became interested in your messages and started tracking when they appeared, to see if there was a pattern (at first I thought they appeared randomly—once every six to eighteen days). Then just by chance I noticed a rather stunning correlation between the appearance of a new message and a documented UFO sighting somewhere in the world. For example:

MONDAY, 19th: New posters along Bloor between Dufferin and Christie. UFO sighted over Lipetsk, Russia (disrupts traffic over airport, according to unnamed official).

FRIDAY, 30th: New posters on Bloor between Ossington and Spadina. In Mexico City, a large rotating sphere (Mothership), orange in colour, releases dozens of white spheres and is captured on digital camera by Antonio Ruiz and multiple Mexican citizens.

TUESDAY, 10th: New poster at the Bloor/Gladstone Public Library. Ngunguru, New Zealand—mysterious light formation sighted in the skies above Tutukaka.

I could go on with further examples, but I'm guessing that I don't need to point out this "coincidence" to you. Suffice to say that I am extremely interested in learning more about your organization. Please get in touch at your earliest convenience. You can learn more about me through my blog: www.disclosureblog.net.

✉ Marina

I'm not a spiritual person. I never have been. My parents took me and my brother to midnight Mass once a year out of a sense of tradition. I don't think they enjoyed it, and we certainly didn't. I stopped going as soon as I had a choice. Church gave me a headache. The stuffiness of it. The old-lady perfume. But over time, as everything has fallen away—family, friends, employment, roommates—as my body deteriorates and I sink deeper and deeper into a state of constant pain or worse, agonizing, incessant itching, I've had to open myself up to alternative ways of thinking. It used to be ciggies and beer. Now it's pine bark and bleach baths. I used to have a fast-paced job at Research In Motion. Now I live on disability cheques, and volunteer twice a week at the Humane Society. It used to be rock 'n' roll and hanging at the Horseshoe. Now it's fibro research or Morgellons chat rooms. All of this is to say that your messages seem somewhat relevant to me. I'm not gonna drink the Kool-Aid, but I wouldn't mind finding out more. I'm pretty much at the end of my rope. Maybe you could get in touch?

John

Some people will believe anything, anything you care to tell them except perhaps that humans evolved from apes, although there's ample evidence for that.

There's no evidence whatsoever that alien scientists from another planet came to earth and created all life, but fifty thousand Raelians believe it. They believe that Rael, formerly known as ordinary guy/race-car driver Claude Vorilhon, was visited by aliens, who took him in a flying saucer to their planet and showed him how—a mere twenty-five thousand years ago—they created humans from the DNA of aliens. The aliens then taught him that he is a prophet who must preach the gospel of immortality through cloning.

Members of the No No Hana sect believed that their leader, Hogen Fukunaga, was the reincarnation of Christ and Buddha. They also believed that he could read people's feet (at nine hundred bucks a pop) to diagnose their illnesses. He had a tendency to diagnose cancer and then charge thousands of dollars for his healing services. Hmm.

Mormons believe that God visited their leader, Joseph Smith, in western New York in 1820, and that a few years later he was visited by an angel named Moroni, who divulged the location of a buried book of golden pages on which was written the everlasting gospel.

The Nuwaubians believe that blacks are a supreme race and that whites were created only to serve as slaves in a killer army to defend them from other invading races. They also believe that their leader, Dwight York, formerly known as ordinary guy/singer in the group Passion (now known as a convicted child molester) is an extraterrestrial from the planet Rizq. They believe that women were created long before men, and that each of us has seven clones wandering about. Sounds plausible.

Members of the Ant Hill Kids believed that their leader, Roch Theriault, was the reincarnation of Moses—even though Moses never killed a follower and then tried to resurrect her by sawing off the top of her head and masturbating into the cavity.

Followers of Bhagwan Rajneesh had no trouble believing he was a supreme spiritual guru despite the fact that he'd regularly glide by them in one of his ninety-three Rolls-Royces.

I probably don't have to mention the countless who believe the world was whipped up in seven days, that woman was made from the rib of man, that the son of God was the product of a virgin birth, conceived by a woman and a holy spirit, and that he died and was buried in a cave but then came back to life and emerged from the sealed cave and subsequently ascended to a happy land above the clouds.

And how many believe that injuries and illness, including incurable diseases, can be prayed away? How many believe that thinking positively about events will change their outcome? All of it is absolutely fantastic. So why wouldn't people believe that my grimy, sweet across-the-hall neighbour Eldrich was a prophet or even a god? Of course they would believe it.

The only question was, could I get Eldrich to believe it?

Amy

John received an astonishing number of responses to the flyers. Total strangers would go to the website and bare their souls. It was crazy. Not surprisingly, theanswertoeverything .org attracted its fair share of interesting individuals—everything from a conspiracy theorist/UFO enthusiast to a selftrained exorcist. There were a few New Age granola types and some sad cases who just needed someone to talk to, but also a reasonable number of seemingly normal humans, people with jobs and friends and families who were obviously looking to fill some kind of void. John, of course, thought it was a big joke and disdained them all. He didn't even bother reading most of the posts. He wasn't interested in their comments, confessions or stories, even though he had solicited them. He was interested only in collecting their contact info and getting them to the point where they would show up for a "meeting." He figured that once they had gathered to hear Eldrich speak, his little Church of Eldrich would be born and he could start collecting tithes.

I think he purposefully didn't read the posts because it helped him keep his distance. I read them all. I'm a curious person. I found them fascinating. And while I couldn't relate to most of the people who wrote in, I did feel empathy for them. There were a few I especially felt sorry for. Like this one woman, Heather, who was in a lot of pain, and who I came to really like. It was Heather's posts that prompted me to write one of the flyers and paste it up around town. John uses this to paint me as some kind of cynical early partner in his escapades. But it was never my intention to take advantage of these people. I wanted to help them!

You can be
Forgiven
You will be
Forgiven
Open Your Soul
Pour out your pain
Allow
That space
To fill with
Peace
&
Absolution
Open
Your Soul
To Me Now

theanswertoeverything.org

✉ Heather

Well, I'm back. And since I've come this far, I guess I'm going to tell the rest. Then I think I'll sleep for about three days. OK.

The first six months were normal. Perfectly, wonderfully ordinary. We had a healthy baby boy with all his fingers and toes. Seven pounds, two ounces. We called him Thomas Owen, after Paul's maternal grandfather and my dad. The breast-feeding was tricky. I couldn't make enough milk and we had to supplement with formula, but that was the worst of it. Even the fatigue wasn't so bad. Thomas was a good little sleeper. And I remember it as being an entirely calm and joyful period. We were surrounded by friends and family, and both Paul and I were over the moon with happiness and pride. I think the overriding feeling was just complete and utter contentment. We finally had our sweet little baby. A real family of our own. Life was going to get better and better, and our love would grow stronger and stronger.

Then things started to change. I noticed it long before Paul did, just in the things that Thomas reached for or even looked at. It sounds ridiculous but nobody knows a baby like its mother, and Thomas wouldn't even *look* at the toy cars and trucks that the other baby boys were so keen on and that Paul kept buying or building for him. If you put a toy car in his hand, he would drop it and reach for my necklace or earrings. Even before he could speak and tell me in no uncertain terms who he was and what he wanted, it was plain to see that he preferred pretty things, girly things—jewellery, dolls, anything frilly and especially anything pink. He wouldn't even look at *Bob the Builder* when Paul put it on, but if *Angelina Ballerina* was playing, he would stare, mesmerized, at the TV. And he preferred the company of girls. Right from the beginning. In the park or with the neighbours' kids he always gravitated to the girls. As soon as he could crawl, he'd crawl to the girls. He had no interest in the boys at all. Paul, of course, hated all of this. He accused me of "sissy-fying" our son. That's the term he used. He said I was making Thomas gay, although the word he used was "homo." As if you could make a toddler that way. Thomas was who he was when he was born. I wasn't encouraging him to like the things he liked. But I wasn't depriving him of those things, either. If he wanted to play with my necklace, I let him. If he wanted to crawl over to the girls, I didn't stop him. Secretly I thought that's what it was with Thomas. That he was going to grow up to be that way. But that was before he could talk. As soon as he started talking it became clear to me that something else was going on. Long before anyone else sensed or acknowledged it, it became obvious to me that God had heard my prayers and answered them. God had given me the little girl I'd asked for. But as some kind of cruel rebuke, He had put her in the body of a boy.

Of course, Paul didn't want to accept it. He didn't believe me when I finally broke down and confessed to him about my prayer in the nursery that night. He said it was nonsense and that I was crazy. He said I wanted Thomas to be a mama's boy, that I was trying to make Thomas gay. If only Thomas had been gay! Everything would've been so easy. So different. I'm sure that over time Paul would have come to accept a son who was that way. He loved Thomas more than anything in the world—at least his idea of Thomas. But Thomas was not gay.

He started talking early. At six months he was saying "Dada." At ten months, "Mama." By the time he was sixteen months old, he had quite a lot of words and could make simple sentences. I remember that right from the beginning when I would say "Good boy!" Thomas would say "No, Mama. Good *girl*." He insisted from the time he could speak that he was a girl, and anybody with any sense could see that it was the truth. Before he was even two years old he would get cross and sulky when we referred to him as "he." He used to unsnap his onesies so they would look like dresses instead of pants. He would sit under the dining-room table and hold the tablecloth over his head to pretend he had long hair. He'd do that with his bath towel too. And make skirts with it.

Of course, Paul despised this behaviour. Over and over again he would explain to Thomas the difference between boys and girls. Boys had penises; girls didn't. Case closed. When Thomas realized that this was true, that he had "the wrong body," he became very sad and withdrawn. Imagine waking up tomorrow with your own brain in the wrong body. That was how Thomas woke up to the world. It confused him. And it made him very unhappy. It was horrible to see. He just didn't quite believe it. I think he really believed that it was going to change. When I asked what he wanted for Christmas, he said he wanted Santa to take away his penis. I would find him clawing at it, trying to tear it off. It was crazy and scary. And the older he got, the worse it got. I was afraid he was going to get his hands on a knife. I couldn't watch him every single second. But I had to. There was no more grabbing a quick shower during the day anymore, or even running down to the laundry room. I was too nervous.

We took Thomas to his pediatrician. I won't say his name, but everyone in the community loved him and thought he was the best. He was my sister's kids' doctor. She adored him. And to be honest, for the first couple of years when everything was run-of-the-mill—vaccinations, colds, ear infections—he was perfectly fine. He told us that Thomas might have a condition called gender identity disorder, and that Paul was right, that we had to convince him he was a boy. He said it would be easier for Thomas in the long run if we could get him to accept the biological fact that he was male. He said that most kids with this condition come to their senses and grow out of it, but that if their parents indulged their delusion, the kids would just be worse off and confused beyond repair. He told us to get rid of anything girly that Thomas could get his hands on, and to only allow him boy toys and clothes, and boy TV shows. He sounded like he knew what he was talking about and I trusted him.

Do you want to know how to make a child miserable? Take away everything that child loves, including the playmates of his choice. Then, if you'd care to see complete misery lapse into depression, weight loss, sleep disruption and self-mutilation—

biting up and down the arms was how Thomas expressed frustration—tell the child they have to behave in a way that is entirely unnatural to them at all times. This was Thomas's life in the months after Doctor X's proclamations. It was horrible. Punishing. I couldn't bear to see Thomas suffer, and I couldn't bear the anger and tension and rage that had taken over our home. Paul and I were constantly at each other's throats. I would hiss at him for being too harsh. He would hiss at me for being too lax—which was any time I wasn't treating my four-year-old son like a macho construction worker. Every time I snuggled Thomas, I was glared at as if I were doing something illegal and harmful. It was horrible. And I came to the conclusion that it was wrong. It was just plain wrong. Depriving Thomas of everything that he naturally wanted was depriving him of something vital that he needed. Paul didn't agree. He would say, "You don't give a kid ice cream for supper just 'cause they clamour for it. You give them what's good for them, 'cause you know better." It sounded reasonable on the surface, but it wasn't a proper comparison. It wasn't like we were depriving Thomas of some bonus thing like candy or treats; it's like we were depriving him of *all* nourishment. And, anyway, if your child refused to eat what was "good for them" and was starving to death before your eyes, you *would* give them ice cream for dinner. You'd give them anything to keep them alive.

But I was an idiot. A fool. I was under the thumb of the doctor and my husband and my sister, and I wasn't thinking clearly. If I had been thinking clearly, I would have been proactive. I would have done research. And I would have left. I would have taken Thomas to Toronto and started a new life. In

Toronto we would have been OK. But I didn't do that. Instead, I started sneaking around, sneaking around with my own son. When Paul was out of the house, I would let Thomas be Emily—the name he had chosen for himself when he discovered that "Thomas" was strictly a boy name. He learned this from Thomas the Tank Engine, on TV. Emily was the girl train. So Thomas wanted to be Emily. And because I couldn't stand to see my child wither away before my eyes, I decided to let Emily be herself for short periods of time when nobody was around. At first it was just an hour a day. I'd let her call herself Emily and allow her to play openly with some of the things we had hidden away. But after I saw what a difference it made to her physical health, I started giving her more and more time. It was like watering a plant that's been neglected. I saw my child coming back to life.

Eventually, I decided to let Emily be herself whenever Paul wasn't around. It was our little secret. The secret world of me and my sweet daughter. The best moments of our lives. I bought her a Barbie doll and started making clothes for it. I taught her how to knit. We would hide everything in the bottom of a garment bag that hung in the back of my closet. For Emily's fifth birthday, I promised I'd take her to get a dress—a real one, not one of my blouses tied at the waist with a bathrobe belt. There was a terrible snowstorm the night before, but she was so impossibly excited that I decided I would dig out the car and we would inch our way to Walmart. Of course, she picked the pinkest, frilliest dress they had. And I bought her matching pink shoes. I can tell you honestly that I've never seen a person happier about anything in my whole entire life.

As miserable and withdrawn as Thomas was, that's how joyful and exuberant Emily was—equal and opposite. She was practically bouncing out of her car seat on the way home. And the second we got in the house and made sure the coast was clear, she jumped into her outfit and ran to the mirror, where she stayed for the longest time, staring at herself. Her honest self. It was a big moment for her. She wasn't playing dress-up with Mommy's clothes. This was the way it was supposed to be. A little girl, dressed like any other little girl. And with her soft curls and dainty features, she looked just like any other girl, except even sweeter and more beautiful.

She said, "Mommy, take a picture of me!"

She wanted to preserve it. She wanted proof of the thing that was being denied. The real and true thing. And so I did. And then we heard the front door open. Paul's noon inspection was cancelled because of the storm. So we stripped off the dress and shoes, and I jammed them in the closet while Emily pulled on pants and a sweater. Then we flew downstairs, where Paul was waiting with a special birthday present for Thomas— two NHL steel hockey nets for the backyard rink. And he tried not to look totally peeved when our child just scowled at the gift, and he bundled up Thomas and took him outside to help shovel the snow off the rink, even though Emily really wanted to help me bake the birthday cake—an activity that was, for her, obviously prohibited. And the rest of the afternoon was the typical tense charade, and I expect everything would have gone on as usual if I hadn't forgotten to erase the photo of Emily from the camera. But I was flustered and I did forget. And when I carried out Thomas's birthday cake—white and blue icing only, no flowers—Paul was waiting in the dining room with the lights dimmed and the camera in his hands. And he turned it on and saw what was there.

"What is this?" he said, fiddling with the camera buttons, breathing hard. I stopped moving. "What the fuck is this?" he screamed. "Are you out of your mind?" He threw the camera across the room and as it sailed by my head I flinched and pulled the cake against me. It slid to the floor and Thomas started wailing.

"It's OK," I said. "It's OK." I tried to go to him but Paul blocked me. "No, it's not OK!" he shouted. "It's not fucking OK!" I'd never seen him so enraged. "What are you trying to do? Are you out of your head?" Thomas was screaming for me and trying to get to me, but Paul snatched him up and carried him upstairs. I chased after them, but Paul slammed and locked the bathroom door before I could get there. I heard Thomas shrieking and Paul yelling at him to hold still. I pounded on the door and said I was calling the police. I ran to our bedroom, grabbed the cordless and ran back to the hall. I was dialling 9-1-1 when Paul came out of the bathroom and knocked the phone out of my hand. He was holding the big scissors.

"Where is it?" he said, dragging me toward Thomas's room. He's a big man and I'm a tiny woman, but I scratched and bit my way free and ran back to the bathroom, where I saw my sweet child on the floor, sobbing, covered in all the hair that Paul had chopped from her head.

"It's OK," I said. "It will grow back." I just almost had my hands on her when Paul grabbed me from behind and pulled me away.

"No. It won't grow back! You have defied the doctor and you have defied me! YOU ARE DONE WITH MY SON!"

I think this is what scared Emily most. It wasn't that Paul forced me to reveal where the dress and shoes were. It wasn't that he took those things and burned them in the fireplace just hours after Emily was finally allowed to possess them. No. It was the idea that Daddy was taking over and what that meant. Clearly, Daddy was in charge and Mommy was powerless to do anything about it. Daddy was strong. Mommy was weak. Daddy put Thomas in his room and wouldn't let him out, or Mommy in. When Mommy kept trying and trying to get in, Daddy picked up Mommy like a rag doll and threw her into her bedroom and wouldn't let her out either. We were prisoners. And Daddy was the guard who patrolled the hallway, at least until three in the morning, which is when Mommy finally gave up and cried herself to sleep.

It was just after six when I woke with a sick, jumpy feeling in my body. I think I half expected Paul to still be standing in the hallway. I listened at the door and didn't hear anything, so I opened it a crack and saw him asleep outside Thomas's room, with sheets and towels from the linen closet as a makeshift bed and all the phones in the house gathered up and tucked around his neck and chest. Paul was the world's soundest sleeper, especially when he'd only been out a few hours, so I knew I could walk by him into Thomas's room without rousing him. And I did. It was the scream that woke him up.

A blast of freezing air. The bed empty. The window open and the screen pushed through.

I knew even before I looked outside that my life was over.

The autopsy report said it was blunt force trauma to the head—a contusion and hemorrhage caused by the jump to icy concrete. But I know what it really was. It was a tyrant father and a feeble mother.

It was my child risking everything in an attempt to save me, when it should have been the other way around.

My biggest mistake of all.

So here I am in the underworld. Too ashamed to live and too scared to commit another major sin.

Emily is with me. I insisted on that and no one dared argue. Her ashes are here on my bedside table. I picked the prettiest marble urn I could find.

A pink one.

Eldrich

The people were broken but full of hope.

I remember the first gathering. John called it a social. Amy made party sandwiches. Pinwheels and lemonade. They moved their tables onto the rooftop patio.

It was grey that morning. Overcast and cool. But as the guests began to arrive the sun burned through the clouds and lit everything bright and yellow. There was a tremendous warmth then. And that's what I remember most. The warmth. The handshakes, the smiles, the happiness of the people coming together on a fine autumn day, sharing thoughts, connecting, finding common ground.

I had doubted John to that point. I doubted his vision and the website and the party. At times, I confess, I even doubted his motives. Most of all, though, I doubted his confidence in me. I didn't think I could be the conduit for God's wisdom and love and assistance—not on any scale that went beyond the tiny and personal. But as I moved through the crowd, meeting old friends from the park and greeting new ones who had found us through the website, I felt an overpowering warmth from without and within. I felt that whatever John's ideas or motives were, God had guided him. A plan was unfurling.

There was sadness too on the patio that day. I could feel it below the cheer and the warmth. A subterranean pain. But there was hope. The people were broken, but they wanted to be fixed. Despairing and hopeful. Beautiful in disrepair. I felt God's love flow through me, and I knew for certain that what was occurring was correct. For the first time in my life, I sensed that my destiny was beginning to unfold as intended. I no longer had that vague tug of a feeling that I was waiting for something to start or to happen.

It was happening on the patio that day. It was starting.

~

Griffin

The journo gods work in mysterious ways.

They giveth: One of the Answer Institute victims used to live in my rooming house. Drew Woollings. A sad little fucker from Brampton. Pimply. Pale. Passive aggressive. We shared a bathroom for nine months before he ran off to join his cult.

And they taketh away: Woollings, one of a small number of Institute survivors (and the key to my story/success) was now in hospital in a coma and largely unresponsive.

My source could not be tapped. Not immediately anyway.

Still, I was lucky. While my former classmates were toiling as unpaid interns in circulation departments, selling the odd tidbit for a pittance to *Exclaim!* or giving it all away to the Huff Post, I had been offered five grand for my first piece. A cover story, no less, in *T.O. Magazine*. A glossy piece. A long one.

My ex-instructor was floored when he found out. Impressed and, I suspect, a little jealous. "If you get this right," he said, swallowing hard, trying to look delighted, "they may put you up for a National Magazine Award." Then he said the beers were on me. What a cock. I had this one shot (plus a mountainous student loan), while he had a steady teaching gig and summers off to make even more money with his thoroughly-competent-but-entirely-boring compositions. Whatevs. I was planning to pay anyway, since I'd invited him out. After that he kept checking in on me, offering to read and give feedback. I told him thanks but no thanks. I didn't need his nicotine-stained fingers in my pie. I told him it was under control. I didn't tell him that the editor was working me like a fucking mule, that I'd rewritten the first third of the piece five times and was still receiving copious, and what I considered condescending, notes. I think the editor disliked me. I think he would've turfed my ass if I didn't have an angle. But I did have one, a sweet one—an insider's view of the life of a dupe in the months leading up to disaster. Yup. The journo gods were smiling when they made Drew Woollings my housemate. Who would have guessed that enduring nine months of Post-it Note tsk-tsks on various bathroom surfaces, and a seemingly endless John Mayer soundtrack, was going to be worthwhile?

But there I was, fresh out of J-school, birthing a five-thousand-word feature about Drew and the demise of his cult. Of course, the editor demanded an exclusive, eyewitness account of the tragic night in question, and wanted select details about the leaders, which meant that buddy boy would have to wake up and spill to me and only me. I called the hospital daily and visited regularly, but he just lay there, eyes wide shut (open on occasion, but not processing). He scored an eight on the Glasgow Coma Scale. Not hopeless, but not exactly peachy either. I would have to wait. And so would the editor.

I thought it would be prudent to get Drew's massive mom on my side, and it was easy to do. Doreen fucking loved me after about five minutes. Of course, she didn't know I was a journalist. You should have heard her rip into the "jackals" who kept trying to get at her and Drew. I found her anti-CBC rants particularly hilarious. I just went with what she assumed—that I was nothing more than her son's old roommate from 262 Jarvis. His buddy Griffin. The only pal who cared enough to visit him in hospital. The guy who was such a true friend, he actually went to the trouble of doing research on comas (I had to figure out if Drew had a chance of ever coming around). So who do you think he was going to open up to when/if he managed to communicate again? The ravening reporters in the hall, the dreaded CBC lefties he'd probably heard Mommy whinge about his entire life—or his former housemate, the guy who brought Mama Bear her coffee and Timbits and Best Beach Bodies in the Universe magazines, the dude who literally held her slab of a hand during more than one tearful bedside vigil, and taught her all about coma stimulation therapy?

I had it worked out.

The only hitch would be if the poor bastard never woke up. Or if he woke up too fried to even blink me a story. Time is the enemy of the coma patient. The longer they make like an end table, the less likely they are to reanimate and recover. It had only been four weeks for Drew, but the clock was ticking hard. And not just for him. Time was the enemy of the newbie journalist too.

If I had any hope of filling those shiny pages with my words, I had to get the story going, pronto.

PART II

John

I set up a website. Nothing fancy, just a little tool to kick-start my experiment and get Eldrich's tosh to the wider world. I made it interactive so that Eleanor Rigby and her ilk could make contact if they wanted to. Amy figured I'd get plenty of digital silence or maybe some guff from bored teens, but I suspected that if I put out just the right kind of signal, just the right kind of individual would pick up on it. Like a dog whistle, if you know what I mean.

It worked.

We started to get hits. At first just one or two a day, but then a few more. And people began to post things. Bizarre things. Hilarious things. Shameful and heartbreaking things. You couldn't make the stuff up if you tried. Amy and I would lie in bed and read through it together. Then we'd fool around. Eat. Read some more, respond to missives, maybe formulate new Eldrichy spiritual messages. I have to say it was a truly interesting period. One of the most pleasurable ever.

I remember feeling that Amy and I had gone deep, fast. She had nothing to do with the art world but was surprisingly simpatico with me. More enjoyable than any woman I'd been with, actually. She loved to loaf. She was a great cook. Smart.

Funny. Expressive in bed. And while I was initially put off by her bony angles, I grew to really appreciate them. There was an odd grace in her thinness—like a giraffe with stick legs and stretched neck, striding across the Serengeti. I loved to watch her move. Elongated and pale. Everything she did looked good. She'd Swiffer the living room and it was modern dance. She had this apple-green scarf she used to wear a lot. The colour combo of the orange hair, the blue eyes and that bright green silk around her throat is something I won't forget. Generally speaking, it was a superb interlude. I was well-fucked and -fed, and art installations were exploding like popcorn in my brain. One post that really stuck with me from the early days came from a hoser who accidentally killed his mother's dog when he was a kid. The unlucky bugger was still tortured by it twenty years later, still dreamed about the pooch every night. I could envision snippets of text from his confession on the gallery wall, then a line of police-style Polaroids of the event stretched out under the words, or circling a video screen with a Guy Maddinesque interpretation of our man's guilty dog dream playing in a loop (black and white, murky, ethereal doggie ghost, etc.), and maybe some artifacts spread out across the gallery floor: the mutt's collar, the ugly bathmat he expired on, the mother's tear-stained hanky. I was itching to make it. But it would have been hugely unethical.

When I set up the website, it wasn't to fish for stories. I didn't want to exploit people. Not in a highly personal way anyway. I just figured we could attract a bit of extra cash and maybe a few more casseroles each week, which would free me to work on MAMA. Eldrich was the sharing kind. If he was benefiting, I would benefit. I wasn't trying to generate material. I was actually against that idea. There was an artist I knew who placed a personal ad in the dating section of the paper and then had a confederate secretly record her café meetings with potential partners. Unbeknownst to these unfortunates, she displayed the whole thing in an Ossington gallery—emails, photos, video, the works, and all the hipsters gathered to chuckle. I hated it. I hated her for doing it. I didn't want to be the smug jackass who would do anything like that. So I decided to detach from the personal tales. They were too creatively distracting. I wanted to make MAMA. That's what I had to focus on. I needed to control the experiment but not become an integral part of it.

I asked Amy to take over the correspondence. I jokingly appointed her director of communications for what I began to refer to as "the Institute" and asked her to print out and file any posts that came in. I would review them at some later date. She pretended to be all concerned with the morality of the endeavour but at the same time embraced her enhanced role with zeal. She was constantly checking the site. She couldn't stop checking it. It was the first thing she did in the morning and the last thing she did at night. I would find her, in the hours in which she usually vegged in front of the tube, online, absorbed, corresponding with the flock. I know it was more fun when we were reading together, and Amy still wanted to, but I had to disengage. Whenever she tried to share, I told her I didn't want the stories or the details, just the numbers. I was aiming to invite roughly forty individuals to the first social— hoping for twenty to actually show, and then for ten of those to "stick." Eldrich already had about a dozen followers, so I told Amy to let me know when we had a solid thirty online. It didn't take long. It took hardly any time at all.

Meanwhile, I had been slowly working on Eldrich, playing the good disciple—asking for advice, borrowing his *Bhagavad Gita*, accidentally letting a copy of *The Teachings of Don Juan: A Yaqui Way of Knowledge* slip from my backpack, and just ostensibly exploring my "cosmic self." Eldrich, I have to admit, remained unimpressed. He seemed closed off. One morning we were enjoying a breakfast doob in his apartment when I decided to lay it all on him. I started by thanking him. A deep and heartfelt *gracias*. I told him how much his words of wisdom and guidance had meant to me. He didn't seem to buy it. When I told him he had set an example for me and had placed me on a path of spiritual awakening, he smiled as if he could tell I was full of crap. But when I hauled out the big guns and assaulted him with the sobbiest sob story of my life, he came to sit with me on the sofa and stared acutely into my orbs (his own brimming with moisture and compassion). I went full force then, concluding the attack with my own waterworks, at which point he covered my ears with his hands and pulled my head against his neck (salt/patchouli), his chin resting firmly atop my head. We sat there for a truly crazy amount of time before he saw fit to release me.

I told him he had a gift, a special talent for healing and helping other humans. "Think about it," I said. "Mindy, Alexa, your friend with the watch, Joyanne . . . all those people in the park, they come to you for spiritual direction."

Small nod.

"Me . . ."

No response.

"What? You think you don't help me?"

"I hope I *can* help you, John."

"You have already, Eldrich. And I think you could help others. And I think if you know you can help, you should. It's almost a duty."

Mulling.

"You're a man of God, are you not?"

"It depends what you mean by 'God.'"

"A powerful, loving force in the universe."

Nod.

"And you've found a way of living through God that you believe to be the correct way to live?"

"Yes."

"So don't you want to share that?"

"I do already."

"But don't you think God would want you to share it with as many people as possible?"

"I believe the people who need to find me will find me. And I'll find the people I need to find." He squeezed my hand.

"OK . . . But what if a person who found you wants more people to find you?"

Eldrich paused for a long time. "Why?"

"Well . . . I just think your message is important. Life is short. People are searching for the right way to live. People could benefit from learning what you know. I've benefited from it, and I want to help others benefit from it."

"How?"

"I was thinking of setting up a website."

I could feel the room grow colder. My words were liquid nitrogen. Eldrich returned to his chair. He stared at his feet.

"Strictly to connect with people," I said. "Just to get the stuff you talk about out there. Maybe provide links to some of the books you've recommended?"

"That's your thing, John."

"Well, it's mostly your thing, isn't it?"

"No. My thing is to do what I'm doing. But if you want it to be your thing, that's fine. I'm not going to stop you from doing your thing."

"OK."

Oh well. It was a start. At least he hadn't put the kibosh on my plan. I thanked him and told him he had touched my heart, and for the first time in a long time I felt hopeful. He didn't entirely swallow it, but he didn't look displeased either.

In fact, when I left him he was sitting noticeably straighter in his wicker throne.

Eldrich

Every man has his secret sorrows which the world knows not; and often times we call a man cold when he is only sad.

Longfellow said that. The poets know the Truth.

Amy

I didn't have a lot of contact with Eldrich early on. As per John's instructions, I would print posts from the site and slide them under Eldrich's door. We weren't sure if he was reading them or not. One morning, as I was doing this earlier than usual, the door opened and there was Eldrich, standing there in his gotch. I found myself almost at eye level with what looked like some very big business stuffed into a pair of formerly white, now washed to oblivion pinkish-grey Stanfield briefs.

"Hey," he said.

"Hey," I said, scrambling to my feet. "John asked me to . . ." I gestured to the pages on the floor.

He nodded. Scratched his stomach. For someone who never seemed to do anything but sit around or lope along, he had a surprisingly muscular belly. And nice hair placement.

"I didn't wake you, did I?"

"No," he said with his simpleton grin. "Want tea?"

"Um, no thanks, I have to—" I pointed to my door across the hall.

"It's already made," he said, standing aside and gesturing for me to enter. "Dragon fruit zinger."

"Oh. OK." I was flustered, trying not to look at his crotch or dwell on the words "dragon fruit."

I went into the living room, which was basically the same as mine but with the furniture arranged haphazardly, or seemingly not arranged at all. There were a million plants everywhere, and the sun was streaming in through the east-facing windows. It smelled like pot and tea and wet soil. Fecund. Pleasant. He must have just watered. There was soft piano music playing on an old-fashioned record player, and the small *pops* and *clicks* of needle on vinyl made a rich, soothing sound.

It was very peaceful until Eldrich came in with my tea and proceeded to sit cross-legged in this tall Addams Family–type chair directly across from the low vinyl sofa where I was seated. Here's the thing: he still hadn't put any clothes on. Once again, I was almost eye level with his package, but now there was no escape. Or no escape until I finished my tea—have you ever tried to guzzle hot tea? What's worse, sitting on the ottoman between us was a stack of junk mail and on top of the pile was a glossy Burger King flyer, advertising a sandwich called the Angry Whopper.

So there I was, drinking dragon fruit tea, with the Angry Whopper directly in my sightline, trying to focus on what we were talking about, which was how long I had lived in the building, what I was studying at school, how I got involved with the website, etc., etc., but I can't honestly remember because the entire time I was really just trying not to laugh, thinking about Eldrich's big old donkey dick and imagining how I was going to tell it to John.

John

Eldrich was full of crap. Which, as it turns out, was great for me. In the days leading up to the first social, he was still playing the taciturn card—*This is your thing, John. This isn't my thing. I'm far too modest and retiring to ever become involved in a thing like this.* To be honest, I wasn't even sure if he would show up to our little party, and had no idea if he'd been reading the website posts or not. I emailed him the link at least half a dozen times, and even went so far as to jam hard copies of website correspondence under his door, but whenever I tried to talk to him about anything to do with the site or its users, he would get all vague and cagey. He would change the subject. Nevertheless, on the morning of our first official gathering, there he was, right on time, looking like Jesus Christ in a billowing cotton tunic, hemp genie pants and sun-baked Birkenstocks, pressing the flesh and welcoming the flock like a good guru should. He seemed to know all the people and their tales of weird.

Eldrich, obviously, had been reading all along.

Amy invited forty individuals to our rooftop party (thirty-one from the website), and twenty-nine showed up. I invested a hundred of my own bucks for refreshments, and within ten minutes every plate was picked clean. No one seemed to care though. Even super-rich dude, who was probably used to the snazziest catering, appeared content with a handful of Cheetos and a plastic tumbler of lemonade. I finally got a chance to meet the guy. He introduced himself as "Phil," but I later learned that his real name was Chen Xi Quan and that he was originally from Singapore. He was short and pudgy, with sallow skin and teeth all askew in blackish-purple gums—like a cemetery after a mudslide. He had no chin to speak of and large, oddly gelatinous eyeballs that reminded me of cloudy aquarium water that needed to be cleaned. He was an affable fellow, though—instantly chummy, with a high-pitched, giggly laugh. When I asked about his watch, he whipped it off and handed it to me to examine. "Parmagiani Fleurier," I said, reading the brand as I strapped it on my wrist. "Interesting design."

"You see it when you're driving." He pointed to the face on the side of the cylinder, and mimed holding his hands on a steering wheel.

"Ah."

"It was a good deal," he said, trying hard not to smile. "Only a hundred and eighty-seven thousand."

This was a routine he evidently enjoyed performing. Now I was supposed to play my part, i.e., gasp with disbelief and either pretend to walk away with the treasure or tear it off as if its very value were burning my flesh. But I just stared at the thing, seemingly unruffled. "Well," I said, "it's a pretty nice wristwatch." In other words, what a colossal waste of cash, you dunderhead. He seemed to get my inference. As I handed it back, he told me it had actually been a gift from his father, who saw him admire it in a store once. "He thought it would make me happy. Nice things don't make you happy."

Ordinarily, I would have said, "But they don't make you *unhappy*, do they, bro? Not like crappy old things that break down and actually incite misery." But given the circumstances, I just nodded in agreement and said, "Eldrich has some very profound insights on happiness."

"Yes," he said, giggling and squeezing my upper arm. "You're a good-looking fellow."

The non sequitur threw me for a moment. I laughed loud and was about to say, "That's what Mama tells me," but he was already moving away when my mouth found the words. I saw him give Eldrich an effusive high-five and a great big hug, then he took off, though not before slipping something into the donation box I had set up by the patio door. Later, when Amy and I emptied it, we found a dozen toonies and loonies, a few crumpled fives and tens, and one very crisp hundred-dollar bill. Amy was all excited. And equally piqued when I told her I was keeping the cash to pay for expenses. She refused to have sex with me that night, even though I assured her there would be many more donation boxes to empty in the future. Whatever. I took the stiff hundred-dollar bill and slid it into my wallet—a colourful woven thing that one of my ex-girlfriends had bought in Guatemala. It looked good in there. Like a business man on holiday.

I decided that "Phil" was a swell guy, and I would get to know him better.

Amy

The first meeting was a pain in the butt. Even though I was back at school and already extremely busy, I was somehow charged with making pinwheel sandwiches for forty people. Fun fun fun. John promised to help, but all he did was pay for supplies and help me carry stuff home from the corner. Then he fucked off to some screening of a friend's short film, while I spent the day up to my elbows in egg, tuna and salmon salad. The apartment reeked for a week. The sandwiches looked pretty, though. I make great party sandwiches.

I think John's original intention had been to hold the event at Eldrich's place, but Eldrich wasn't exactly down with the plan in the early days, so that wasn't going to happen. Then John tried to persuade me to have it at our place, but I refused. Who knew what kind of degenerates were going to show up? Did I really want a bunch of spiritually starved sociopaths tracking bedbugs into my apartment? No thank you. I thought we should just do a picnic in the park where Eldrich usually busked—familiar, safe, easy to disperse if things got weird— but John thought it wasn't official enough. Also, he didn't want to attract attention from suspicious Mommy types—especially if some super-freaks decided to attend. I compromised and said we could hold it out on the rooftop terrace, as long as he agreed that nobody could use the bathroom in our apartment. And if it rained, tough luck. No one was coming in. He grudgingly agreed.

Almost everybody who I invited showed up. Unfortunately, Heather, the one person I was actually hoping to see, didn't make it. We'd been corresponding through the website quite a bit, and even though we'd never met, I considered her a friend. She was traumatized by the loss of her child and was suffering from PTSD, but she wasn't totally bonkers like some of the others. Wayne, for example, our UFO nut job, who arrived with a big-ass SLR digital camera and proceeded to photograph all the satellite dishes on the roof of our building and the buildings around us, as if they were picking up alien messages instead of the latest episode of *Modern Family*. Or dippy Anne-Marie, who insisted on greeting everyone forehead to forehead so she could feel their energy. Or wild-eyed Tyson who was completely covered in religious tattoos: a giant crucifix that started on the back of his neck, then sprouted elaborate wings all across his shoulder blades, Jesus Christ nailed to the cross and bleeding all down his left arm, and another Christ—this one in extreme close-up with a woeful expression and a blood-dripping thorny crown, on the right arm. He also had GOD'S SOLDIER tattooed as a kind of word bracelet, and a pair of realistic-looking hands clasped in prayer, with rays of light shooting out all around them, on the side of his tree-trunk neck.

Can you say "crazy-town"?

Eldrich took it all in stride, though, and seemed to adore everybody. There was a lot of hugging. Far too much hugging for a group of people who had never met before. And there were a few uncomfortable minutes when Eldrich jumped atop a plastic milk crate and recited a fable about a young man who stood in the centre of town, boasting about his beautiful, perfect heart. All the villagers gathered around to marvel at his pristine muscle. But then an old man approached and said that his tattered and torn heart was the superior heart because it was missing pieces that he had given away, and because it was scarred from emotional upheavals, blah blah blah. All the villagers scoffed and turned away. But the young man saw that it was true, and wept, and tore a piece of his heart out and put it in the old man's heart and they walked away arm in arm. Or something like that.

I was fully expecting *our* villagers to scoff and turn away, but instead everyone erupted into applause. And this one guy named Drew actually started blubbering like a baby and didn't stop until Eldrich went over and cradled him in his arms. I remember thinking: *The freaks have found each other . . . and it's on my terrace. Super-duper.*

John, of course, had a grand time. First he wolfed down half the sandwiches that were intended for guests, then he spent the rest of the party stalking (and flirting with) Phil Chan, Eldrich's wealthy benefactor. Poor Phil. John had him wound around his finger from the get-go.

After Phil left, John seemed eager to wrap things up. He had set out a donation box and was obviously dying to see what was in there. Phil had very generously donated a hundred-dollar bill, which John swooped up like a hawk with a rabbit. He said it was for the food, but I was with him for the shopping and couldn't help but notice that he'd only spent seventy-two bucks and change. He took the rest of the money—fifty-six dollars—to pay for web hosting, and the postering he had done. He said we would hold another gathering soon, and that, because of all my help, I could keep half the proceeds of that. I told him I didn't give a shit about proceeds, but I wasn't making any more pinwheel sandwiches.

I have to say, it was kind of bizarre how jazzed John was by that hundred-dollar bill. I think it gave him an actual hard-on, since he put the cash in his wallet and then immediately tried to mount me on the living-room floor. I found his monetary excitement off-putting. Plus the apartment stank of chopped egg. I think that was the first time I didn't want to have sex when he initiated. And maybe the first sign that we were very different people. Anyway, a few days after our initial gathering, Eldrich came by and asked me to show him how to log on to the site to post. That's when he started putting messages directly on the splash page. That's when he began corresponding with his people.

Friends, Tender Hearts, Explorers . . .

Life is a gift. Seekers such as yourselves know this. Others who are less aware squander the gift through misuse or, more commonly, under-use. Some even throw the gift away.

Our greatest goal is to make the most of the gift. To do this, we must find our Absolute Self—not who others expect us to be, not who society says we should be—but our true, authentic self. Only as our Absolute Self can we commune with the All Powerful. But how do we do it?

Can a seed take root in a quiet garden? Yes. Can a seed take root in a roiling sea? No. Can our Absolute Self take root in quiet contemplation? Yes. Can our Absolute Self take root in a flurry of emotional gyration? No. Just as we wouldn't toss a seed into a whirlpool and expect it to grow, we can't expect our True Self to grow in a vortex of regret, bitterness, anger, blame, self-recrimination, intolerance, unforgiveness, guilt, shame, desire, or self-consciousness. These toxic elements poison our waters. We must purify to find stillness and see our true selves reflected.

Let us purify together.

Your Absolute Self is waiting to be discovered.

With love and optimism,
Eldrich

John

I celebrated Eldrich's first website post in the most appropri-
ate way I could think of: with a bag of Meyer lemons and a
bottle of vodka. Amy and I got rightly hammered on my very
cold, very excellent martinis (straight up, with a citrus twist).
She danced interpretively (pretty) to the new Tom Waits (wild)
and then let me do things no woman has let me do before. A
memorable night.

I think it's safe to say that we discovered our *Absolut* selves.

Amy

Eldrich was a joke to John. A very useful joke.

I admit that Eldrich's early website posts were a bit airy-fairy, maybe a tad exalted. But there was usually something in them, something true and compelling. To me, anyway. John thought they were complete rubbish. He said that Eldrich never really said anything, or just said the same vague spiritual thing over and over again, which is why they worked. And, oh man, did they ever. Our hits went up exponentially when Eldrich took over the postings. That's when we got our first visitors from outside Toronto. That's when we first heard from Mushroom Steve.

✉ Steve

Dudes/Dudettes, my name's Steve. Nice to virtually meet you. I'm in the Peg right now, but I'm originally from Quebec. I think I must be the first person ever to move from Montreal to Winnipeg. :) It's usually the other way around. When people ask about it, I say I needed to find a worse winter, so it was either this or St. John's. :) Seriously though, there was some personal BS that I needed to escape, and since I have family in Alberta, I decided on Manitoba. Ha ha! But seriously, I'm not into that whole cowboy, pickup truck, oil-sands vibe. I like Winnipeg. It's comfortable. I can wear my pyjamas to the store and no one notices or gives a shit, right? But I've been here a couple of years now and I'm thinking it's time to push on. More BS. Surprise, surprise. I have a part-time job in the kitchen at Thai Origins, really good people, good food, but I've been seriously thinking of checking out the Centre of the Universe. :) Burned some bridges in Vancouver a while back, so I think Toronto's my next destination. I see you're headquartered there. I've been reading all the comments about your recent open house and it sounds like it was pretty frickin' cool and good vibes all around. Are you having another one soon? My guess is I'll probably be splitting in the next week or so, so maybe you can let me know. It's freakin' freezing here, dudes! We got snow already. Yesterday was minus twenty-five. OK. I'll keep checking the site. Peace out! mistersteve23@yahoo.ca.

✉ Eldrich

Dear Steve,

Our next meeting will take place on Saturday, November 12, at 55 Hawton Blvd, apartment 1203. You are most welcome. Please join us. We will be having a potluck luncheon beginning at noon and ending whenever we grow weary of connecting and discovering.

You are loved.

Eldrich

John

The second gathering was kooky and kind of great. We had nearly sixty sweaty Seekers, all bearing macaroni salad or mini-marshmallow brownies or some such toothsome treat, crammed into Eldrich's apartment. In a matter of weeks we had doubled our attendance. And thanks to my inspired conception to make the get-together a potluck, we had leftovers for days, including one particularly fine batch of homemade beet-leaf *holopchi*, crowned in a creamy dill sauce and transported all the way from Winnipeg by our first long-distance convert, Mushroom Steve. Insert hearty lip-smacking sound effect here.

"Phil," alas, didn't show. According to Eldrich, he had to undergo some kind of medical procedure. At one point, Eldrich hushed the crowd—including the spillover sardine-ing in the bedroom, kitchen and hallways—so we could all take a moment to send positive, healing energy to our "dear friend." Everyone dutifully stopped mingling/masticating, fell silent and focused on . . . what? I grudgingly paused midway through a red velvet cupcake and scanned the room. Everyone had their eyes clamped shut. I felt thrillingly alone until I spotted Amy in the corner of the dining nook by the didgeridoo, looking back at me. We smiled at each other and it was a crackling good moment of connection. We were both amused and amazed by the folly we had fashioned. With my eyes locked on Amy's, I went to work on the cupcake, thickly and lasciviously tonguing up a dollop of pink icing. She averted her gaze, shaking with stifled laughter. Eldrich's "moment" of healing silence went on and on. I was about to quietly unbutton and waggle my cock, when some hapless schmo—I think it was crazy Wayne—flushed the toilet in the bathroom and spoiled my antics (and possibly Phil's expedited recovery).

"Thank you, friends," said Eldrich gravely from his wicker throne after the plumbing-interruptus, and at that very moment, as if he were a cunning Vegas magician with a confederate waiting in the wings, his cell phone began to vibrate and spew the opening bars of some indie hipster hit. "It's Phil!" he announced, beaming at the synchronicity of it. "He says the procedure is done and he's tired but fine!" A self-congratulatory cheer went up around the apartment as if the motley throng had personally scrubbed up and performed a delicate surgery. I tried to exchange a contemptuous smile with Amy, but she wouldn't meet my eye.

She was cheering along with the rest of them.

Amy

It was the second meeting, the one at Eldrich's, that catapulted things to the next level. Mushroom Steve came, but I don't remember him specifically because it was crazy crowded and I was talking mostly to Heather. I know he was there, though, because he left his calling card in the donation box—a home-made paper and Scotch tape envelope with enough psilocybin inside for two. John wanted us to try them together, but I said no thanks. He got pervy enough when he was drunk. The last thing I needed was him hopped up on hallucinogens, trying to maul me in some weird way. Guess what else was in the donation box that day? Nine hundred and seventy-two dollars. Almost a thousand bucks. We couldn't quite believe it. It made no sense. The funny thing was, after the first meeting, John was all like, *You can keep half the proceeds from the next gathering, Amy, 'cause of all your wonderful help and support.* That changed, of course, as soon as he saw what was in there. Suddenly he was like, *We have to start a bank account* and *We should look into getting charitable status for this thing.* He suddenly realized the potential of what he had started. Here was a way to make money that was a lot easier and more reliable than applying for grants and then waiting five months to find out if he could survive for the next six on a pittance. It was a potentially more lucrative thing too, judging by that one afternoon's haul. That's when John started talking about holding meetings every Saturday. That's when he started asking me, or more accurately *begging* me, to take a year off school to help him run the thing. And that's when he set up the Twitter account and persuaded Eldrich to start tweeting.

TheAnswer2Everything
@AnswerInstitute

TheAnswer2Everything 🐦
@AnswerInstitute

Allow your soul to breathe and smile. Allow your soul to laugh.

theanswertoeverything.org

14 Nov

TheAnswer2Everything 🐦
@AnswerInstitute

Imagine the light inside of you growing brighter and brighter and brighter.

theanswertoeverything.org

16 Nov

TheAnswer2Everything 🐦
@AnswerInstitute

Inhale energy. Exhale pain. Inhale light. Exhale darkness.

theanswertoeverything.org

17 Nov

TheAnswer2Everything 🐦
@AnswerInstitute

You are the only you. Do not conform. Confirm.

theanswertoeverything.org

18 Nov

TheAnswer2Everything 🐦
@AnswerInstitute
Extremes excite. But tranquility and happiness reside in the centre of all things.
theanswertoeverything.org
18 Nov

TheAnswer2Everything 🐦
@AnswerInstitute
In stillness there is peace. In peace, truth. In truth, freedom.
theanswertoeverything.org
19 Nov

TheAnswer2Everything 🐦
@AnswerInstitute
You are loved. The heart of the universe beats for you.
theanswertoeverything.org
20 Nov

TheAnswer2Everything 🐦
@AnswerInstitute
Father, Mother, Child, Wife, Husband, Friend, Teacher, Judge. The One you need is all this and more.
theanswertoeverything.org
21 Nov

TheAnswer2Everything 🐦
@AnswerInstitute
Your True and Absolute Self is waiting to be born.
theanswertoeverything.org
22 Nov

TheAnswer2Everything 🐦
@AnswerInstitute
Together we will wash away regret. Together we will vanquish pain.
theanswertoeverything.org
23 Nov

TheAnswer2Everything 🐦
@AnswerInstitute
Tomorrow is new. Your pristine future starts now.
theanswertoeverything.org
25 Nov

John

Eldrich invited me to tag along when he went to visit Phil at home. It was November but strangely warm and humid—some kind of record high for that particular date in Toronto. On the way, Eldrich confided that Phil had recently been diagnosed with cancer. The docs didn't know how bad it was; the surgery he'd had was an exploratory laparoscopic procedure to see what was what. I thought he looked unhealthy when I met him.

We took transit to his place, which was up around Lawrence and Leslie, a very chi-chi neighbourhood, with some of the most expensive and offensive homes in the city. We ogled our way past a vast display of energy-gobbling mega-mansions before finding Phil's street and his surprisingly modest-looking home. After the watch and the Bentley, I was expecting something grandiose, something pillared, but 81 Elderbrook looked like it could exist in any middle-class, mid-century Toronto suburb. The front lawn was wide and deep, as was the driveway, which started straight, then arced slightly to the left into an ordinary two-car garage. The house was a bungalow and seemed on the small side for any neighbourhood but especially diminutive among the Bridle Path behemoths. It proved to be an optical illusion, though. Once you entered the home, you got a sense of its true size. The foyer was expansive, with highly polished oak floors and a huge leaded-glass skylight. Basically, all you were seeing from the curb was this foyer, jutting forward from the main building and flanked by trees. Once inside, you could see how the building extended back and widened out. It was easily three thousand square feet of living space— small for the area, but still schmancy—and all hardwood and marble and thick Persian rugs.

Phil seemed happy to see me. "Handsome! Hello! Thank you for coming!" He was dressed oddly in bell-bottom lululemon yoga pants, a Tommy Bahama sweatshirt and a knitted cap and scarf. He led us into the kitchen, where we sat on bar stools at a large granite island while he unpacked a delivery he had recently received from a gourmet grocer. There were a dozen or so salads, each with an outlandish price sticker: $9.00 for a tiny tub of roasted beets, $11.65 for a sprinkling of couscous. There were exorbitant cheeses, high-end crackers and— I'll never forget this—a slim box of organic popped corn that had been "hand-produced at exactly 479 degrees Fahrenheit." OK. I ate the contents in three handfuls. We drank midget bottles of Limonata that had been über-chilled in a special beverage drawer built into the island. I downed three of them in short order, much to Phil's amusement.

"I wish I had your appetite," he said, moving some orzo around on his plate and sighing.

The plates all matched and so did the cutlery. My fork weighed half a pound. I think it was made of platinum. We used linen serviettes.

"I'll clean up here," said Eldrich. "Why don't you relax?"

"Thanks," said Phil. "I'm still a little woozy from my sleeping pills." He moved to a massive leather sofa in the adjoining family room, covered himself with a throw blanket and patted the seat next to him. I trotted obediently to his side and sank into a sofa cushion. I asked for his story, and he gave it to me.

Phil, originally monikered Chen Xi Quan, was born and raised in Singapore. His family was still there and was one of the richest in the country. He said they were in the hotel business, but I later found out that in addition to owning seven hundred hotels across Asia, they owned a prominent bank. He told me they were also involved in Singaporean politics. Phil, middle child of three, was the pink sheep of the family—exiled to Canada after announcing to his parents that he was gay (bad) and wanted to come out (very bad), and intended to marry his Muslim Malay boyfriend who was nineteen years his junior (impossibly, stupendously, intolerably bad). The family could not abide the shame and ridicule of such a thing, so they paid Phil to change his name and disappear from their lives forever. They paid him a lot. He didn't say how much but indicated that it was more than he could ever lavishly spend in a lifetime. "Put it this way," he said. "They made sure I would never come back for more." He laughed his giggly, high-pitched laugh, but he didn't look so happy about it. His boyfriend, Mat, didn't mind a bit, though. Phil said he was positively tickled to leave Singapore with a mountain of cash. At the time, there were a handful of countries where same-sex marriages were legal. Phil and Mat considered Spain and the Netherlands, but eventually decided on Canada because of its proximity to the US. The couple liked to frequent New York, so they opted for Toronto over Vancouver. Phil's family arranged for citizenship, and Phil and Mat moved here and got hitched. Fifteen months later, Mat withdrew $800,000 from a joint bank account and fucked off. Phil had set up the account so Mat could dip in freely and feel financially independent. Bad idea. A private investigator tracked him to Venice, California, where he was living freely and financially independently with an underemployed actor/personal trainer. Phil could have (and I think, should have) called the police and US Immigration to recover both Mat and his dollars, but he decided just to let it all go. He said that if Mat had married him for the money, he didn't want him back. And he didn't need the dough, so that was that.

We talked a bit about his illness. Phil was pleased that the outcome of the exploratory surgery was relatively positive. There had been some question as to whether his cancer was too far gone for him to even receive treatment. If it had spread to his liver, for example, he would have had to manage the cancer instead of attempt to eradicate it. Now, even though it was more advanced and widespread than the doctors had hoped, Phil was at least eligible for surgery to remove the various tumours. But because there were only a handful of surgeons in Canada who were trained to do the finicky procedure he required, Phil had been told that he would have to wait two months. Of course, the rich don't wait two months or any months. Phil promptly booked himself the surgery at

Memorial Sloan Kettering Cancer Center and a suite at the St. Regis for the four weeks of post-op recovery. Eldrich offered to go along, but Phil said he had friends in New York who would rally around him, one of whom promised to find a hunky male nurse to come to the hotel every day.

"But maybe you could house-sit for me while I'm gone?"

"As you wish," said Eldrich.

I wanted it to be me. I wanted it to be me. "I could mow your lawn," I said with a hint of lewd, as if I had instead volunteered to ream his ass.

He laughed. "Here's a guy who obviously hasn't seen my lawn!"

"That's a good idea," said Eldrich. "It's too nice to stay inside. Today is a gift. And vitamin D is important."

"What about my wrinkles?" squealed Phil in mock protest, allowing himself to be led like a child by the hand to the backyard.

And then I understood. Here was where the grandeur of the house lay. This was where the Singaporean hotel and bank money had come to roost—in the impossibly vast ravine lot that extended back forever to the edge of an actual wood (or 690 feet to the periphery of Wilket Creek, according to Phil), where a massive old oak stood like a sentinel.

"Holy crap!" I said, gobsmacked. "This is incredible."

We had walked out onto a large, furnished deck with two separate seating areas, a wood-burning pizza oven and the Bugatti Royale of barbecues—a stainless-steel corner unit flanked by beer fridge and ice machine. The deck led down to a wide expanse of lawn and garden—beyond which lay a swimming pool and cabana, then more lawn—before angling off to one side, toward a giant tennis bubble, then even more lawn and finally, finally the woods. It was an oasis. A paradise. All shielded from neighbours by a natural fence of thick, tall evergreens. A secret, magical place.

"Still want to mow my lawn?" Phil giggled.

In answer, I bolted onto the grass and, stirred by fine weather and the open stretch of green, turned my first cartwheel in about twenty years. I ended up on my back, staring at the sky.

"Handsome, don't hurt yourself!" Phil laughed.

Eldrich vaulted over me, like a hurdler, and bounded, long-legged and gawky, toward the pool, where he began to strip off his clothes.

"Your pool is still filled?" I said, moving toward the blue shimmer.

"Open all year," said Phil. "I heat it to eighty-four in the winter and swim when it's snowing."

I was equally appalled and enthralled by this information. Here I was turning off lights when I left a room.

Eldrich leaped into the water, and I contemplated doing the same until I saw his thickly skid-marked undies lying on the ground. I kicked them out of sight, and then chose a highly designed padded lounger to recline upon. The fabric was warm and smelled toasty. Phil shuffled over and stretched out on the chair beside me.

"You're not going to swim?" he said.

"Are you?"

"No. No energy."

We were quiet for a few minutes, feeling the sun, watching Eldrich dart back and forth under water. A regular Johnny Weissmuller.

"Mmm," said Phil, enjoying the warmth. He doffed his cap and unwound the scarf from his neck.

"You a tennis player?" I gestured to the white dome near the end of the yard.

"No. That was there when I bought. I'm going to have it removed."

"Really? You should try playing. When you feel better. It's a great game."

"I took lessons when I moved in. I don't like it. The court is all in horrible condition."

"Mind if I have a look?"

"Go ahead. I'm going to dig it out next spring. I like basketball. Maybe I'll put in basketball courts."

"You play basketball?" It was amusing to imagine.

"I'm good at basketball! I could beat you, handsome!"

"Them's fightin' words, Phil."

"I've been playing since I was little."

"You're still little."

Phil mock-punched my arm. "I'm five feet three inches! Muggsy Bogues is five feet three inches!"

"All right, Muggsy. You and me next spring."

"Next spring," said Phil with a wistful sigh.

"You'll be fine," I said, patting his leg and getting up. I went to check out the tennis court. Phil wasn't lying. It was in awful shape. The surface was cracked beyond repair and resembled a dried-up riverbed. Countless gangly weeds sprouted from hundreds of asphalt vaginas. The nets had been taken down and heaped in the corner. It was just a big open space. A big, entirely unused space, one with a skylight and a bar fridge and a two-piece bathroom attached to the entrance.

Perfect.

A wave of excitement fizzed through me as I headed back to the pool, cartwheeling my way across the long, long lawn.

Amy

It was around then that everything moved up to Elderbrook. Initially, it was to accommodate Phil, who was suffering from a rare form of stomach cancer. Our third gathering was scheduled to take place on a Saturday in late November, which was the day before Phil was flying to the US to have surgery at a private hospital. Eldrich had a plan for his send-off—a mass "laying on of hands" that was supposed to convey healing powers from the group. It sounds loopy, I know, but Phil was into it. He just didn't like the idea of having to head to Eldrich's cramped apartment just before his trip, so John suggested that the meeting be held at his house instead. I was all for it because I wanted to check out his place. John, who had already flirted his way into Phil's luxe life, had been going on about how amazing it was. So I was curious. And even though I sort of knew what to expect, I was surprised when I saw it. The home itself was lovely—not a mansion but wonderfully spacious, and appointed with all the best high-end features and finishes. The lot was incredible, though. Like nothing you'd ever expect to find in the city. The backyard was pretty much a private park—huge, secluded and ridiculously deep. There was a giant deck, a flagstone patio, a beautiful pool, endless amounts of lawn, a tennis court, even woods and a creek. It was like being at a cottage or somewhere out in the country. It smelled crisp up there. Fresh. No trace of exhaust fumes. Just oxygen. And plenty of room to breathe. It was the perfect setting to hold meetings of a spiritual nature. Much better than our cruddy apartments on Hawton Boulevard. The only downside was that it was in the middle of nowhere. Up in North York around Leslie and Lawrence. Not at all convenient to get to by TTC, and with a pretty long walk after you got off the bus. I remember it was pretty miserable weather the day we first met there, cold, grey and windy. I figured people wouldn't make the trip, that it would just be us and possibly crazy-town Tyson or weepy Drew Woollings, but nearly everybody from the second meeting showed. And there were additions—Anne-Marie brought her teenage son, Richard, and Joyanne brought Perry and Moina, an old hippie couple who used to make experimental films back in the 1970s. Eldrich, apparently, was worth the trek.

The Elderbrook meeting seemed more structured and official than the previous ones, but we didn't plan it that way. I think it just happened because of Phil's basement. The former owners had completely transformed the place to look like an old-fashioned movie theatre. There was a carved wooden stage with a panoramic screen and a heavy red velvet curtain flanked by wooden pillars. The curtains opened and closed automatically, just like in a theatre. It was pretty cool. And there were rows and rows of padded, flip-down seats that had been salvaged from a defunct movie house at Ossington and Bloor. At the other end of the long room was a cute snack bar with a working popcorn machine and groovy vintage tin signs for different items. *Mr. Dee-lish Hot Buttered Popcorn. Mountain Dew, It'll Tickle Your Innards! Chilly-Dilly—The Personality Pickle.* Everyone had been milling around the snack bar, grazing on trays of sushi and Thai salad rolls, but when it came time to get people's attention, Eldrich naturally took to the stage and everyone naturally ended up in the seats. It wasn't like Eldrich was trying to be big man in the spotlight, it was just the obvious place to address the attendees from. Still, even with him seated cross-legged and being relatively low key and Eldrichy, the proceedings seemed more formal with him raised up and everyone else in the audience.

"Friends, Seekers, thank you for coming today. I love you, and I'm so happy to see you. Welcome to new friends who have come to join us for the first time. And thank you to our generous host, Phil, who has received us into his home and provided us with shelter and sustenance and a comfortable place to convene."

A smattering of applause. A wave from Phil in the front row.

"Some of you travelled a long way on buses and subways to get here. When we leave today, could the people with cars please give the people without cars rides home or at least rides to the subway?"

More applause. And Eldrich warming to it. "Emerson said that the purpose of life is to be useful, honourable and compassionate. So let's try to make it easier for each other whenever we can. OK?"

Cheers from the crowd.

"So . . . the last time we were together, we sent healing energy to Phil from a distance. Today we have a chance to intensify the curative process by transferring life force directly from our healthy bodies to Phil's ailing body, which is out of balance. Phil, you want to come up now? I think if you lie right here, then people can stand beside you and it'll be a good height."

Eldrich spread a yoga mat out at the edge of the stage and Phil dutifully stretched out on top of it.

"Is that OK? Are you comfortable?"

"It's good. Yes."

"OK. Maybe we should all take some deep breaths before we begin. Let's focus on breathing in healthy, vital energy and breathing out negative, dirty energy."

Eldrich breathed in deeply and then everyone else breathed in deeply. Eldrich breathed out purposefully and then everyone else breathed out purposefully.

"Cleansing breaths," said Eldrich. "In through the nose and out through the mouth. Think of each breath washing your cells and your internal organs. Think of each breath cleansing your physical body and at the same time brightening your light and shining your soul."

He inhaled. They inhaled. He exhaled. They exhaled. Once rhythm and synchronicity were firmly established, Eldrich began to speak softly.

"The universe is energy. Energy and electricity. Humans are also energy and electricity. Our cells generate electrical impulses. That's what makes the heart beat. Our brains are full of glial cells and neurons. Neurons are like tiny electrical transmitters. We have billions of them in our brains. Literally. Our circuitry is beautiful and complex."

"I will praise you," shouted Tyson, rising from his seat. "For I am fearfully and wonderfully made!"

"Yes," said Eldrich. "Very—"

"Marvellous are thy works; and that my soul knoweth right well!"

"Thank you, Tyson."

"Psalm 139:14," said Tyson, nodding. "Anyone here doubt it? Anyone who thinks we weren't created by a benevolent God?"

Nobody spoke. But a strange sound issued forth from John, in the last row.

"We are fearfully, wonderfully and *intelligently* made," said Tyson, scanning the crowd, as if daring someone to challenge him. Nobody did. We all just stared at his thick neck and his crazy tattoos and his shaved, muscular head. Satisfied, he murmured, "My soul knoweth right well, right well . . .," then lowered himself into his chair.

"OK," said Eldrich. "Maybe we should start. Who wants to start?"

Anne-Marie put up her hand. "I used to do therapeutic touch."

"OK. Cool. Then maybe we should just all line up so we don't have to interrupt the flow of energy to figure out who's next."

Anne-Marie approached the stage, and people shuffled into position behind her. I noticed, as I took a spot between Drew and Catelyn, that John hadn't budged. Heather also remained seated, and I later learned that she felt her energy was too corrupted, too sick to transmit to Phil. Oddly enough, Marina, our fibromyalgia poster girl who could speak of nothing but her myriad mystery ailments (including "alien fibres" sprouting from her arms), was directly behind Anne-Marie, raring to go.

The room was quiet as, one by one, people moved to the stage to either lay their hands on Phil or skim them lightly over his body. Eldrich controlled the length of time, allowing some to linger longer than others. A few were dismissed with a nod after only ten or fifteen seconds. I was hoping to be one of the quickly dispatched. I felt self-conscious and awkward, mostly because of John. I could feel his eyes on me. I could feel his judgment and scorn. I am not an airy-fairy person, and I don't appreciate being viewed as such. I am a scientific person, and I happen to know that the brain-body connection is powerful. It's real. I knew that what we were doing would, at the very least, be psychologically beneficial to Phil, and that what is psychologically beneficial is often physiologically beneficial. Even if we were just helping Phil to relax, we were, in fact, serving him. And so I took my place in the line and went to the stage and did the deed. I hovered my hands just above Phil's body and passed them slowly back and forth from his head to his feet. Eldrich kept me there for what, at first, felt like an excruciating amount of time. But after a few minutes I forgot about John and being embarrassed and I just eased into the thing, into the motion and the purpose of it. I felt a strange warmth and tingle in my palms and fingers as they floated back and forth through what seemed like a substance thicker than air. It became hypnotic and calming, and I lost myself for who knows how long. It was only when Eldrich touched my shoulder that I regained the room around me. As I was returning to my seat, I noticed that John had taken off while I was up there. So I pretended to need the bathroom and went to see where he had got to.

I found him in the tennis bubble. He was drinking beer and unpacking building materials for a massive sculpture he planned to construct. He had convinced Phil to let him use the defunct space as an art studio for as long as he wanted. Obviously, John felt zero compunction about exploiting a cancer-ridden man who was at his most vulnerable. But he thought it was just fine to make me feel like an idiot for actually trying to help that man.

"Ah, there she is: *reiki master*." He said it with a Japanese accent. He bowed.

"That's funny stuff."

"You know about the guy who invented reiki, right?" He swigged his beer and belched. "The whole healing touch thing?"

"No. I don't know anything about him. But I guess you're going to tell me."

"Can't remember his name, actually. But the important thing to know is that he died of a stroke when he was sixty." John laughed.

I let him have his little victory, then I said, "Presumably you've heard of the placebo effect?"

"You think that's what's going on in there?"

"I don't know. I haven't conducted any long-term clinical studies. I suspect that's what's happening. But I don't claim to know everything about everything."

"I see," said John. "You're open-minded." He said it with derision. He said it with air-quotes.

"Yes, I'm *open-minded*. Now gimme a fucking sip of that."

"There's more," he said, gesturing to the fridge. "Grab me a fresh one."

I should have told him to get his own freaking beer. But I didn't. I fished out two cold Steam Whistles. John twisted the cap off his and flicked it across the tennis court. "You know that Dawkins quote about being open-minded?"

I sighed.

"'Let's be open-minded, but not so open-minded that our brains drop out.'"

"Ha ha."

"You think Anne-Marie believes she's administering a placebo? You think Tyson thinks that?"

"No. Obviously not. That guy's frightening."

"Yeah. If God were so benevolent, would he have given dude a neck that's wider than his head?"

"Funny."

"I can't believe Phil's subjecting himself to such mishegoss."

"What difference does it make? Phil's happy about it. It might look weird, but there's no harm in it."

"I wouldn't be so sure about that."

"So helping Phil to relax is harmful?"

"I don't know. It was making me sick to watch it."

"Oh really?"

"Yes. I got dizzy. Felt like I was going to hurl."

"Yeah, well . . . you started this."

"Yeah, well . . . maybe it's time to end it."

"Now that you've got your patron. And your free studio. Who paid for all these materials?"

John didn't answer. He drank his beer. He smiled. "Ever get fucked in a tennis bubble?" he said, moving in on me.

"We should get back."

"Take your pants off."

"No."

"Come on," he said, tugging at my belt loop. "I'm sure Eldrich has got it covered."

"No . . . it's not that."

"Then what?"

"Urinary tract infection."

"Jesus. Another one?"

"Yeah, well . . . we've been having a lot of sex, you know. All kinds of sex . . . and all it takes is the tiniest bit of E. coli bacteria to get in there."

"Hmm. So much for being 'wonderfully and perfectly made.'"

"Thanks a lot."

"Nothing personal. I'm just saying an intelligent designer never would have put the cunt hole so close to the ass hole."

I had to laugh.

"The vadge should be here." He gestured to his belly button. "The asshole should be clear the fuck on the other side. Like right at the tailbone. Or better yet, at the bottom of the foot. Vadge where it is, but shit-hole at the bottom of the heel. Food goes from the stomach, down the leg and out the foot. That would be a far more intelligent design, don't you think?"

Silly, yes. But I guess he had a point.

Eldrich

A transformation. An awakening. An ancient key delivered in a mysterious way. A young woman decides to venture out. A neighbour with a need for a roommate. A fresh face across the hall. A thirst. A hunger. Disclosure (loss). Embrace. Endeavour. The striving. The outreach. A technological tool. A tweet from afar. A journey of a thousand miles. The missionary. The messenger. A guide with a gift. The sacred flesh. The withered phalli. Teonanácatl. God's mushroom. God's flesh. The taking in. The cracking open.

Revelation.

Transcendence.

The new Eucharist.

John

So Eldrich does 'shrooms with Steve and everything goes wonky up at Elderbrook.

Instead of nibbling psilocybin, then blissing out to tunes or giggling their asses off or staring at mirrors or their own hands for hours on end, Eldrich and Steve gobble half the stash, then go gallivanting around the property, beseeching God to "reveal himself," chanting and moaning, rending their garments—one moment dancing like sprites, the next solemnly summoning "the Creator" to appear. Unamused, I roll pickles in turkey slices and retreat to my bubble to sup and work on MAMA. (Did I mention I was given the tennis court to use as a studio over the winter?) I find the boys later, zonked out of their gourds in Phil's crazy-ass, egg-shaped marble bathtub, writhing like snakes against the dry stone. Eldrich—in just undies and socks, Steve, *sans* trousers and sporting an irretrievably shredded "Neutral Milk Hotel" concert T. This appears to be more of a sensual than sexual affair. Their hands palm the smooth marble surface as they squirm and grope, Helen Keller–like, feeling and feeling, grinding their hot faces against the tub's cool interior.

"Gentlemen," I say, taking hold of the Estée Lauder Youth Dew bath oil and the Pink Peruvian Infusion Crystals, "could

I prevail upon you to relocate? It is time for Johnny's bath."
I've been hanging in Phil's master ensuite almost every night.
The marble egg is a superb soaking tub. Just the right angle
for comfortable reclining, with or without a book. I make the
water almost unbearably hot, pour in a cocktail of perfumed
unctions and steep until shrivelled. Amy sometimes joins me,
but on this night she's at home, trying to catch up on school
work. I haven't been home for a week.

Although they appear uncomprehending, Steve and
Eldrich oblige, slithering out of the tub and skittering across
heated marble floors into the bedroom. I don't encounter
them again that night.

The following afternoon, I find Eldrich seated cross-legged
atop the granite island in the kitchen. He is sporting a paisley
silk robe that is four or five sizes too small (Phil's, obviously).
He informs me that not only did he see God on the previous
evening, he briefly *became* God. I congratulate him as I thaw a
rib steak to grill for my lunch (barbecuing in the snow makes
me strangely happy). Eldrich concludes that his messed-up
state on psilocybin was "the true reality" and that the generally accepted, run-of-the-mill version is actually a "hallucina-
tion." He is caressing a kiwi when he tells me this, stroking its
soft sides with an index finger, as if it were a pet, as if he were
a Bond villain. When the microwave *dings*, he cocks his head
like a chicken and laughs incongruously.

Gradually, over the next couple of weeks, Phil's peaceful
suburban retreat becomes an open-all-night drop-in centre
for the congregation and their stray associates. Mushroom
Steve is Eldrich's faithful acolyte. They seem inseparable,

wandering and pondering, administering to the flock, conducting "research" on Phil's computer or having frequent breath-holding competitions in the swimming pool (why they do this, I do not know).

Phil, meanwhile, lies feebly in hospital, recovering from an all-day surgery, oblivious to the fact that his house is being overrun by maniacs, including a green-eye-shadowed creature named Catelyn who has actually moved in with her daughter (after being threatened by her ex, ostensibly), setting up camp in a guest bedroom. Garbage bags full of clothes and toys abound. I feel uneasy about this state of affairs, but Eldrich assures me that Phil will be "cool" with it. He tells me that Phil is behind the Institute 100 percent. When I suggest that Phil's support likely doesn't extend to secretaries and their toddlers taking up residence, he leads me deep into Phil's bedroom closet (which, I feel the need to share, has three fucking skylights in it) and fishes out an old photograph album from a mahogany pocket-square drawer. Inside is an envelope, containing a legal document. It is a signed amendment to Phil's will, which basically states that should he die during his procedure in New York, or in the year following his return to Toronto, his house (and sufficient funds to pay required taxes, and legal and transfer fees) will be left to the Answer Institute, provided that it is used as headquarters for the organization, and that Eldrich sits on the board of directors.

"See," says Eldrich.

But I don't see. My heart is doing a Buddy Rich–on–timpani imitation. "Um . . ." I say. "I know Phil is going to be fine—"

"He is," says Eldrich. "I *know* he is."

"But just in case—"

"He will be," says Eldrich with his wise-man smile.

"No, I know, I know. The operation was a success, thank goodness."

"They think they got all the cancer."

"That's great. Thank God!" I pause here for a moment. "But considering what's at stake . . . and given that there's still the tiniest scintilla of a chance that something could go awry—"

"It won't."

"No, I hope not. But Phil *is* in a very weakened state, right?"

"Yes."

"I mean, you haven't actually spoken to him, have you?"

"No. I'm in touch with his friends."

"Then I think it can't hurt to err on the side of caution. Because if anything did happen to Phil, this would be meaningless in a court of law." I wave the amendment at him. "I mean, I think we need to respect Phil's wishes, and that means we should probably consult a lawyer. We should probably make the Answer Institute legal and official as soon as possible. Just in case."

Eldrich gives me a funny look.

"I know you're not into the organizational stuff, and that you'd prefer to keep everything open and organic, and not in any way corporate, and I agree. I mean, I'm an artist, not a businessman. But honestly, in this case, I think we need to act. If only out of respect for Phil."

"It's OK," says Eldrich, patting my knee. "It was taken care of. Right after Phil left."

"Oh," I say, trying to sound casual. "By who?" I'm thinking Mushroom Steve is an evil genius. He shows up with his psychotropics and his beard braids, and everyone thinks he's some dumb-ass hippie. Meantime, he spied an opportunity and he fucking seized it.

"Amy," says Eldrich. "She's good at all that business stuff."

"Amy?" I said, not quite grasping this info or its implications. "*Amy* had the Institute incorporated?"

"I figured you knew."

"No . . . she didn't mention it." Punch in the gut. Lungs squeezed by invisible hands.

"I guess she's been super-busy with school."

"Yeah, I guess she has."

"She hasn't been around much."

"No, she really hasn't."

"Are you all right?"

"Yeah."

"You sure?"

"I'm fine," I say. But I'm not. I've just been torn from my accepted reality, the waking dream in which Amy and I are together. A unit. I flash on the last conversation I had with my father. He is urging me to trust no one (before my mother grabs the phone away).

"Anyhow," says Eldrich, sliding the paper back into the envelope and the envelope back into the photo album and the photo album back into the mahogany pocket-square drawer, "I wouldn't worry about Catelyn moving in for a bit. I'm sure Phil wouldn't mind."

"You're probably right," I concede. It's not Catelyn I should be worrying about.

Amy

December was a total nightmare for me. I had multiple papers due and two exams to study for, and I was stupidly behind on everything because of my work with the Institute. Oh, and to top it all off, I was cat-sitting for my parents, who were in Arizona looking for a vacation property. And I wasn't even allowed to bring Jasmine to my place—that would be too traumatic for her—so I had to trek out to the Beaches every day to feed and pet her. Forget cleaning my apartment or getting a badly needed haircut or even thinking about Christmas shopping. That stuff wasn't even on the table. I was going almost around the clock, getting about four hours of sleep a night. I had sacrificed a ton of my study time for the Institute, but instead of being thanked or appreciated, I was attacked. Now, I know that John likes to paint me as all cutthroat and conniving, but the fact is, I was only trying to protect Eldrich and Phil. Eldrich asked for my help, and I responded in a way that felt most correct in my gut.

I'd also like to point out that I never initiated anything. *Eldrich* came to *me*. After Phil left. He was upset. He confided that Phil had laid a huge responsibility at his feet, and he was feeling uneasy about it. He didn't want to have to handle it on his own. What happened was, just as Phil was getting into the limo to go to the airport, he handed Eldrich an envelope with a surprise inside. Essentially, Phil had changed his will and was leaving his house to the Institute if he were to pass away during surgery or in post-op. Phil was really very sick. It wasn't beyond the realm of possibility for him to die during a twelve-hour surgery. I knew that if this unfortunate turn of events came to pass, we would be in a huge pickle, given that Phil was still legally married and that the Institute was not in any way an official entity. His home was worth between three and four million dollars. People have killed for a lot less, right? Can you imagine the endless courtroom battles that would ensue over something like that? It would be frickin' Bleak House, assuming we weren't just tossed out at the onset. I suggested to Eldrich that the smartest thing to do was incorporate the Institute immediately. Then at least we wouldn't be embroiled in quite such a litigation hell should anything tragic occur. He agreed with me. He agreed 100 percent. And he asked me to handle it. He had no idea how to do it, and he asked me to do it. So I did. To save money for the Institute, I dealt with it myself, online, without the aid of a lawyer or accountant. It's a pretty fiddly process, and it took me about a week to make it all happen, a week in which I could have—and should have!—been focusing on my school work. But did I get any props for my sacrifice? No. Just the opposite, in fact.

John, who had made himself cozy up at Phil's place as soon as Phil left for NYC—even transporting his air mattress out of our apartment and into the tennis bubble—showed up at home one night, all pissed off and accusatory. Oh wait, no.

First he came in and quietly ate everything that was left in the fridge, and then he got all pissed off and accusatory.

"So . . . what's new and exciting?" he said. "Anything to share?"

I knew instantly what he was getting at. The way he phrased it. His posture—arms crossed, pelvis thrust forward. The half-smile.

"Anything you'd like to fill me in on?" he added.

"The file's right there," I said, gesturing to the red folder on the coffee table. I turned back to my work. "In case you haven't noticed, I've been a tad busy lately."

"Yes," he said, scooping up the paperwork, "you've been very busy, haven't you?"

"Yes, I have. *Extremely*. And it's not like you've been home at all. It's not like we've had a chance to chat about what's going on."

"True. I have been far, far away in the wilderness of Lawrence and Leslie. How could you possibly reach me up there in the outer limits?"

Snide. I didn't respond.

"A thirty-second phone call or a ten-second text message would've been much too much time out of your schedule to alert me to a development as trivial as this."

"Look at me," I said. "*Smell me*. I haven't showered in two days. I haven't eaten hot food in a week. I've got a brutal exam in the morning, and I've had four major papers due. This is not some big subterfuge or secret. OK? If it were, would I leave the freaking documents lying out on the table? I mean, you *are* still living here, are you not? Or have you officially moved into Phil's place now?"

"So you planned to tell me about this, you just didn't have the time to call or text?"

"That's right. Now, do you mind if I get back to my work?"

"Go ahead. You don't mind if I have a look at how you structured things, do you?" He sat beside me on the couch and opened the file.

"Knock yourself out." I tried to focus on my reading but had to keep restarting the same paragraph as I braced myself for the tirade.

"Wow. This is interesting," he said. "You've made yourself secretary, treasurer, chief executive officer *and* chief operating officer."

"That's very typical," I said. "Do you know anything about incorporating? I had to do this as quickly as possible. If you're not happy with it, we can change it."

"And Eldrich is president. Nice. You didn't want to be prezzy as well?"

"Funny."

"You know what the really funny thing is . . . I don't see *my* name anywhere in here. You and Eldrich appear to be the only shareholders in this entity."

"In case you haven't noticed, Eldrich and I were each allotted 250 shares. There are *one thousand* shares available. I left room to add you later."

"Oh that's big of you. But if Phil kicks off tomorrow, you and Eldrich own his house, don't you?"

"No. The *corporation* would own it. The Answer Institute would own it. And it would be used as Phil intended, to carry on Eldrich's work."

John laughed.

"And your insensitive reference to Phil 'kicking off' makes me think I did the right thing."

"So you admit you intentionally excluded me?"

"Look, I had to get this done as quickly and efficiently as possible. I didn't have time to call you up and start debating all the minutiae. I left room for changes. It's easy to change."

"But you just said you did the right thing by excluding me. So which is it? Efficiency or bloodsucking greed?"

"What? *Greed?* Oh my God! I was trying to honour Phil's wishes!"

"Right. This from the woman who trolls the MLS every night, drooling over granite countertops and hardwood floors."

"Um, hello! If I were trying to steal Phil's house, why would I have divided shares equally between me and Eldrich? Why wouldn't I have given myself more shares, more control? It's not like Eldrich even asked to see this."

"I don't know. Maybe it's easier to settle for half a giant estate than to have Eldrich raise a stink over a whole estate?"

"Uch, you're full of it! And if that's what you think about me, we're done." I stormed off to take a piss. John followed me to the bathroom. He softened his tone considerably then. He obviously wasn't ready to be done. Suddenly, he was all puppy-dog eyes and wounded feelings.

"OK. So, you wanted to honour Phil's wishes. Fine. I believe you. But why didn't you include me? I thought we were a couple. I thought we were in this together."

"We are. And I'm sorry, I just—I guess at the time I was thinking of the worst-case scenario. If Phil dies, what happens to his place? Who is going to honour his wishes, and who is just going to take advantage?"

"That's a very good question."

"Hey, I'm not the one sponging off the guy! And you know as well as I do that you think the Institute and Eldrich are full of crap."

"But you don't?"

"No, I don't. I think there's truth in a lot of what Eldrich says."

"When there's real estate involved, you're a believer?"

"Uch, I have to study!" I pushed by him and went back to the couch. John stayed in the bathroom. I heard the shower start. A full half-hour later, he emerged, steamy and naked, his dick plump and swinging. He had obviously fluffed it up to show off.

"Look," he said, "I'm sorry. And you're right, if anyone's behaviour has been suspect, it's mine. I have accepted supplies from Phil, and the use of the studio. But that doesn't mean I wouldn't honour his dying wishes. Phil and I are pals. I really dig the little guy."

"OK," I said. "And you know I feel the same way, right?"

"Yeah. And you are the one with the open mind. I shouldn't have doubted you."

"You know I've always admired Eldrich for trying to help people. I actually like a lot of the people. Heather especially. And Drew's really sweet."

"Seriously? He looks like the pimply virgin who shoots up the school."

"He's actually very nice and very eager to help out. Not that you've gotten to know any of them . . ."

"Oh, I've gotten to know them. Especially in the last two weeks. I've seen them in their pyjamas."

I laughed.

"C'mere . . ." he said, opening his arms. He opened those strong arms and invited me in. He looked good. He had the kind of body I like. Thick.

"I stink," I said, moving into the damp, warm embrace.

"I don't care." He held me tight and whispered hot into my ear, "I'm totally going to fuck you."

At the time I thought it was pure sex, and exactly the stress break I needed, but in retrospect I wonder if he maybe meant it another way.

Eldrich

Nine thousand BC in a cave in the Sahara Desert, a rock painting of a man with one hand on a mushroom and the other on the spiral of life. In the Chapel of Plaincourault, in Indre, France, a fresco of Adam and Eve standing on either side of a magic mushroom tree—the real Tree of Knowledge? Mushrooms depicted in Mayan temples, mushroom statuettes in Aztec ruins. Mushrooms in the stained-glass window in Chartres Cathedral, which illustrates St. Eustace's vision—what could have brought that on? Amanita muscaria. The bread of life. Manna from heaven. Exodus 16, verse 14: *And when the dew that lay was gone up, behold, upon the face of the wilderness there lay a small round thing, as small as the hoar frost on the ground.* A small round thing in the "wilderness"—ancient translation of *wilderness = pasture*—in the morning dew! Verse 15: *And when the children of Israel saw it, they said one to another, It is manna. And Moses said unto them, This is the bread that the Lord hath given you to eat. Manna.* Manna = mushrooms!

John 6:31: *Our fathers did eat manna in the desert; as it is written, He gave them bread from heaven to eat.* John 6:51: *I am the living bread that came down from heaven . . . The bread is my flesh, which I will give for the life of the world.* Jesus's flesh = Amanita muscaria.

Flesh of the gods.

Teonanácatl.

My eyes had been opened and the path forward was clear. The Answer Institute would embrace the holy sacrament and spread enlightenment to all those who wished to be cosmically connected and spiritually reborn. My deepest wish was to begin cultivating and disseminating as soon as possible. Alas, Steve had to start the process without me, as I was summoned by Phil to New York City.

John

You know what they say about flies and honey? So true. But I used a different sticky substance to catch my fly—a wily Diptera who had taken legal ownership of the Institute while I was paying more attention to art than commerce (it is my way). A trip home and a lengthy and tender lovemaking session was clearly in order. I capped it off with a full-body, ylang-ylang lotion rubdown—including ten minutes on each bony foot, after which Amy (unbidden) offered to change the structure of the Answer Institute, Inc., and make me chief executive officer with an equal portion of preferred shares.

No frogmarching required.

We met after her exam the following day and sauntered hand in hand to a wildly affordable, storefront lawyer in the Junction to make the requisite changes. Randolph E. Clapp, LL.B.—knowledgeable, competent, possessing the filthiest carpet I've seen outside of a pub. He sorted it out in short order. *Thanks, Clapp.* Although I was itching to immediately return to work in the bubble, I then accompanied my fly to her parents' house to feed and fondle a dandruffy, foul-smelling cat called (unimaginatively) "Jasmine." This proved beyond a doubt that my doting behaviour had nothing to do with corporate matters, and Amy, who that very day had dispatched with school duties for the season, was high-stepping. After preparing a decent meal of canned vegetarian chili and freshly baked ACE garlic bread, she took me upstairs to see her childhood room. I feigned interest in various knick-knacks and mementoes, tsk-tsked the fact that her sister, Allison, had been given the larger, skylighted room next door, assured her she was far more attractive than this large-roomed sister, beaming from a photo atop the dresser, then plowed her hard on her narrow bed (with Tori Amos and David Bowie staring down at me from postered walls). I was subsequently rewarded with a twenty-minute back tickle complete with Amy's first avowals of *amour* (I was the bestus boyfriend ever), which made the trip to the Beaches and all that fawning over fat, fetid Jasmine entirely worth it.

Did she mean what she said? Who knows?

Maybe it was true that she'd excluded me from the initial incorporation because she felt I was taking advantage of Phil. It could have been true. And at that moment in time, I certainly wanted it to be true. But I honestly couldn't tell. I didn't know if we were two people who really dug each other but didn't quite trust each other, or if we were two people who didn't trust each other an iota and were now pretending to be in love.

Would I have preferred it to be the former? Of course. But was I willing to be a rube?

Trust no one were the last words my father ever spoke to me (before my mom grabbed the phone and said, *No, no, Johnny. Better to be betrayed than a person who can't trust*).

Hmm.

After all the bedroom lovey-dovey, Amy and I went to the

basement and drank ironic whiskey sours—her parents' cocktail of choice—at an actual barlike structure. We played Ping-Pong (be-yotch beat me every time) and likely would have just imbibed ourselves goofy if I hadn't received a call from Eldrich saying that Phil had taken a bad turn. He'd developed an infection that had morphed into septicemia. Eldrich was leaving for New York in an hour. I asked if he wanted me to go with him (shockingly, I still hadn't seen the new MoMA), but he said no, that Phil's caregivers had arranged for one ticket only and, anyway, he wanted me to return to Elderbrook to supervise the various individuals who were now shacked up there: Mushroom Steve; Catelyn and her daughter, Staci; ubiquitous hippie-dippies Mindy and Alexa; and some acne-ravaged sad-sack named Drew who just that day had settled himself and two dozen plastic boxes containing the entirety of his possessions into Phil's family room. Yeesh.

Poor Phil. I felt bad for the guy, I honestly did. The possibility of him dying became all too real all of a sudden. I thought of him tiny and depleted in a hospital bed, his blood boiling with bacteria. I thought about his giggly laugh, his bell-bottomed lululemons, the way he addressed me as "Handsome." Phil had been very generous with me. And kind. Now he was dying in New York City, with who knows who at his side? I thought of his family in Singapore. Shouldn't someone be contacted? Wouldn't they want to know? How sad was it if they just didn't care? Or worse, if they were relieved?

Amy was on her third whiskey sour when I shared what was going on. "Holy shit," she said, choking on a sip, her eyes widening. She jumped up and started gathering glasses and lemon rinds. "We'd better get back," she said, briskly tidying. She was excited. I could practically hear the hamster wheel spinning fast in her brain as she contemplated the consequences of Phil's demise. I had a flash of Amy taking over Phil's house—propped on fat pillows, eating bonbons in his bed, hanging her clothes in his walk-in closet, redesigning his kitchen with her beloved Property Brothers. I didn't like it. Not a bit.

I knew in my heart I didn't want Phil to die. I said as much to Amy and added: "I think it would be colossally unfair for Phil to expire and have wastes of space like Mindy and Alexa swanning around his house."

"Yeah," she said, distracted. "Maybe we should take a cab? It'll be a lot faster."

"What are you looking for?"

"My purse. It's probably upstairs . . ."

I followed her to the main floor, where she called a taxi ("The Institute can pay, right?"), loaded/started the dishwasher and gave Jasmine a series of overly effusive goodbye nuzzles. Her eyes were bright and her cheeks were flushed pink. She was just tremendously keyed up.

"Yeah," I said as we waited in the vestibule for the taxi, "I hope the little guy pulls through. Does it say anything about survival rates?"

Amy had Googled "septicemia" on her iPhone and was reading keenly. "Hang on . . ." She flicked the screen with her finger to get more info. "Oh my God . . ." she said. "Oh God. This is not good . . . Poor Phil!"

That's what her mouth said: *Poor Phil!* But her eyes seemed to say: *Lucky me!*

Eldrich

.

I knew Phil would get better. I never doubted it. God told me in a vision that was vivid and clear. I was given a dream of Phil, laughing in a forest—a lush, tropical forest. He was eating papaya, swallowing juicy mouthfuls of bright orange fruit and spitting out the black seeds. Orange in. Black out. Health in. Disease out. He was shirtless—lean and muscled now, with criss-crossing scars where the doctors had stitched him up, where he had healed. The sun was shining in golden shafts through the canopy of trees as Phil devoured lusty bites of papaya. Orange in. Black out. And all the time laughing and laughing. I knew he would be well.

Phil's infection happened for a reason.

I was summoned to New York for a reason.

And that reason was Xavier Raine Maddox.

Xavier Raine Maddox
@RaineMaddox

I'm not the captain of the universe's most advanced spacecraft, but I play one on TV.

Xavier Raine Maddox 🐦
@RaineMaddox

Great to be tweeting again! Thanks for all your support and good wishes. It truly means the world!

19 Dec

Xavier Raine Maddox 🐦
@RaineMaddox

The sun is shining & I get to see it! Feeling tired but happy & met the most phenomenal human this morning. #EveryDayIsAGift

20 Dec

Xavier Raine Maddox 🐦
@RaineMaddox

"Our wounds are where the light gets in." Wise words from my new Canadian friend. More here: #FF @answerinstitute

23 Dec

Xavier Raine Maddox 🐦
@RaineMaddox

"It's the injured oyster that produces the pearl." Eldrich = Genius. #FF @answerinstitute

23 Dec

Amy

And then came Raine. Xavier Raine Maddox, who at the time didn't mean much to me but seemed to mean a lot to the sci-fi geeks who watched his show: *Deep Sky*. He had done a detective series—one of those police procedural franchises—a few years before that, and I remember thinking he was hunky whenever I surfed by, but I never watched an episode. And I never thought of him as a giant celebrity. I mean, I would have recognized him as a TV actor if you showed me his picture, but until he got involved in the Institute, I couldn't have told you his name. Imagine our surprise when we suddenly got thousands of followers on Twitter when he #FF-ed us after connecting with Eldrich in the hospital.

Sorry, let me back up here. What happened was, a couple weeks after his operation (after everyone assumed he was on the mend), Phil came down with a serious infection. Sepsis. Full on. Eldrich flew to New York to be by his side. It was pretty touch and go for a few days there. The docs had to devise some crazy cocktail of antibiotics to save his life. But it kicked in eventually, thank goodness, and Phil (who lost twenty-two pounds in the ordeal) slowly came around. That's when Eldrich met Xavier Raine Maddox—in the halls of the hospital. He was there having surgery to remove some pre-cancerous cysts from his pancreas and, over the course of a few days, forged a friendship with Eldrich. I guess Eldrich talked him through a pretty intense time. When I first met Raine, he told me that Eldrich had been sent to him by fate to help him turn his life around so he could start to "live brightly."

Eldrich stayed in New York over the holidays and was a guest at Raine's home a few times. It made me laugh to picture grubby, flannel-shirted Eldrich hanging out in Xavier Raine Maddox's swanky Manhattan brownstone. He was even invited there for Christmas dinner, but Eldrich chose to stay at the hospital with Phil. Raine sent a catered Christmas feast to the room and the nurses' station. Phil sat up that night and even tried a sip of eggnog, and apparently it was a very festive evening and kind of the turning point in his recovery. Pretty cool.

In mid-January, Phil and Eldrich finally returned home. And a few days later, Raine came to visit and attended several meetings, much to the delight of the congregants, who were understandably jazzed to have the rakish captain of *Deep Sky* in their midst—Drew was especially wound-up, following Raine around like an excited schoolgirl, blushing whenever he spoke to him.

So, as it turned out, all of John's angst and anger over me incorporating the Institute was for nothing. In fact, John was grateful I had taken the initiative, since we were about to start generating significant revenues—thanks to Raine's involvement/endorsement—and it was vital to have the business in place to deal with that efficiently.

Of course, that's when John really put the pressure on me

to quit school. He wanted to be in the bubble, working on his sculpture, but he also wanted to take advantage of the opportunity that was presenting itself, i.e., he wanted to capitalize on the exponentially escalating popularity of the Answer Institute. Or wanted me to. Since Phil wasn't entirely sold on having his home perpetually overrun with Seekers—that's the word Eldrich and John seemed to settle on for congregants—it was decided that we would start a building fund with the aim of purchasing a headquarters for the Institute. To that end, John concocted various merchandising schemes: podcasts, DVDs, special seminars, photographs of Eldrich, etc., and he begged me to leave school to help him get everything going. He was very persistent and persuasive. He pleaded, sweet-talked and bribed—he said if I left immediately, I could name my starting salary and give myself a retroactive Christmas bonus. When that didn't work, he took a different tack, basically trying to guilt me into it. He was unbelievably unrelenting, and in the end I caved and withdrew from my course. Not because of the salary and bonus. Not at all. I didn't give a shit about the money, even though I was substantially out of pocket after withdrawing from a course I had already paid for. No, I felt a responsibility to the Institute and to Seekers. John made me feel that it would be a betrayal to head back to school and dump the whole thing in his lap.

I guess it was a combination of feeling accountable and also feeling that something genuinely worthy was happening at 81 Elderbrook. Phil was beginning to heal and feeling happy; Heather, who had been basically catatonic, was starting to show signs of life again—she had totally bonded with

Catelyn's daughter, Staci, and was taking care of her while Catelyn was out looking for work or attending her CAMH meetings; Raine was visiting regularly and attracting some pretty interesting people to the cause; Eldrich had started to write his tracts . . . There was just an upbeat vibe all around—a feeling of community. An effervescence. It was kind of exhilarating to be a part of it. And because I had been there since the beginning, I didn't feel entirely comfortable abandoning it to pursue my own selfish interests / career. John made me feel like a traitor for even contemplating it, so I decided to sacrifice for the greater good.

Would I have left school to work full time at the Institute if John hadn't pushed and guilted me into it? No. Definitely not. I would have finished out my year and then maybe taken a hiatus. But John Aarons could be a very persuasive and extremely convincing person, believe me.

John

Phil survived, and Amy's dreams of no-money-down mansion ownership were dashed. But she was pleased with the souvenir he brought home with him from NYC. A bauble called Xavier Raine Maddox. Never heard of him? Yeah, me neither until he arrived at 81 Elderbrook and the legions started drooling. Dude had been the star of some crud TV show called *Deep Sky*, some Joss Whedon-y sci-fi thing that made the fan boys erect for a few years. I had never seen it. And neither had Amy, but apparently any C-list celeb—even a short, balding, thick-thighed forty-six-year-old—was enough to send her into a jean-moistening tizzy. As soon as Raine came on the scene (and yes, Raine was his real name, actually bestowed at birth, which should give you an indication of his flaky upbringing), she decided to devote all of her being to the Institute. Her chief aim was to bask in Xavier Raine Maddox's celebrity glow (no matter how faint). Her secondary mission was to monetize his connection to the max. Our little psych major started to sound and behave a lot like an MBA. And I admit, buddy boy did attract a bevy of Seekers to our doorstep—so many that we had to consider relocating, which did require a certain amount of planning and administration. Being stupidly rich affords you loads of leeway, but even Phil had to think about his neighbours, who might start to wonder why hundreds would show up to his abode at the same time every Saturday and Sunday, clogging the previously pristine curbs with automobiles dusty, dented and not manufactured in Germany.

I have to guffaw, though, every time I hear Amy's claim that I coerced her into leaving school to run the Institute. What rubbish. A total fiction. I'd never seen anyone embrace an enterprise with such zeal. She was a regular Ron Popeil— dreaming up products to hawk through the website. What's more, I invite all interested parties to please go to York University and ask to eyeball the marks Amy scored on her first semester term papers and exams. All sad Cs and dismal Ds. She was failing the year. She knew it. Her profs knew it. And anyone who cares to check the records will know it.

Amy throwing herself headfirst into the Institute had nothing to do with my powers of persuasion and everything to do with academic deficiency and a lust for luminaries and lucre.

Eldrich

Steve was sent. Then Raine. He brought followers, of course, many Seekers, but he was not just God's magnet or amplifier. No. He himself was a messenger who carried first-hand knowledge of a spirit plant, a sacred botanical from the jungles of Peru. Not a mushroom. A vine. It was this godly vine, *Banisteriopsis caapi*, brewed by shamans into a blessed beverage, ayahuasca, that told Raine there would be cancer coming. Worms swirled around the place where the disease would sprout and grow. Fluorescent-green worms with multiple heads and mouths. The worms told him there would be disease. When he left Peru, he knew he had to act. He told his doctor about the worms, but his doctor didn't believe him. He said that Raine was the healthiest patient in his practice. Raine pushed. The doctor ordered blood tests and urine tests. The blood tests and urine tests came back normal. Raine pushed again, but the doctor sent him away. Luckily, Raine trusted his God-/plant-given vision and not the opinion of one well-intentioned but limited man. He went to a clinic and paid for a CT scan. And the scan revealed the Truth. Raine had precancerous tumours on his pancreas—tumours that would have devoured his life force had he not acted.

Ayahuasca gave him eyes to see. The spirit medicine saved his life.

Raine promised to take us to an ayahuasca ceremony. Or, if Phil was too weak to travel to the jungles of South America, to bring the ceremony to us.

Amy

It got really busy, really fast. There was a growing demand for Eldrich and anything to do with Eldrich. On top of that, we had all the rabid Xavier Raine Maddox fans, who thought they might get close to him at 81 Elderbrook. Seekers, geeks and celebrity hounds were descending on Phil's place, and not just at scheduled meeting times. It was tough for Phil, who was still very weak and convalescing. John and I had to move up there full time to act as gatekeepers and try to keep things under control.

Seekers who couldn't get to Toronto were emailing and posting on the website, and sending in donations. John had revamped the site with the help of Wayne, who aside from being a UFO freak turned out to be a wizard at coding. They set up a PayPal account and changed the splash page so it would show the donations to the building fund growing incrementally. We didn't reveal how much money was being raised, just how close we were getting to achieving our goal, which was secretly, and absurdly—at least I thought so at first—two million dollars. For each ten thousand raised, another virtual brick was added to a cute little animated building in the corner of the page. The first ten bricks came surprisingly fast. Then Phil donated seventy-five thousand and Raine kicked in twenty-five thousand—ten more bricks. And then Raine started tweeting to his followers, exhorting them to donate "a dollar for each beautiful year they had been granted on earth." Soon we had seventy-six bricks, which was pretty shocking if you think about it. And that was just the donations. We were also selling merchandise. Our Seekers Perry and Moina volunteered to film and edit the meetings for us, which they intercut with footage of Eldrich speaking on different topics or answering interview questions. We burned those on DVDs and sold them for twelve dollars each, or nine dollars for a download. We sold eight-by-ten glossy photographs of Eldrich for five bucks a pop. Audio podcasts were ninety-nine cents. To be honest, we were making a ton of money. I mean, the Institute was.

Elderbrook was pretty full at that point. Phil was back in the master bedroom. Eldrich and Mushroom Steve shared the one next to Phil's. Catelyn and her daughter, Staci, were in the third. The fourth was supposed to be kept empty, reserved for Raine's visits, but Heather crashed in there a lot. Drew had moved into the pool house with Mindy and Alexa, who had taken him under their wings. Tyson was in the basement. And John and I were on his air mattress in the tennis bubble. Since Drew was living on-site anyway and super-eager to help out, we hired him as an assistant. He made trips to Costco or Walmart so that we always had provisions—food, bottled water, paper products, bathroom items, cleaning supplies, etc. He was also responsible for making weekly runs to our apartments to water the plants and pick up mail. We gave Tyson a stipend to act as bouncer and scare off star-struck interlopers who were just trying to get to Raine, and he also kept the basement auditorium clean and organized. Heather was given a modest salary to prepare refreshments for the meetings, a task she seemed to enjoy and performed well. Between that and babysitting Catelyn's daughter on weekdays, Heather was really starting to improve. You could tell she was taking better care of herself—the greasy, unkempt hair started to look washed and combed, and then sometimes even styled. Little bits of colour began to appear in her all-black-all-the-time attire. It was good for Staci too. Prior to Heather, she'd basically been stuck in front of a TV all day with her chain-smoking granny while Catelyn was out looking for work or on a bender. Now Heather was playing with her the entire time, showing her how to do all kinds of things: cook, bake, read, knit— Heather was making herself and Staci matching green sweaters with wool from Anne-Marie's yarn shop. It was lovely to witness. They were like two inert elements that when mixed together made light.

You could see how things might have progressed in a relatively normal and successful fashion. We would have eventually raised sufficient funds to relocate to a permanent headquarters. Eldrich's teachings would have continued to spread, attracting more people to meetings (which now had an admission price: a twenty-dollar donation). In a perfect world, we could have been giving ourselves good salaries and helping people at the same time. But the world isn't perfect. Far from it.

I don't know if it was the drugs or the adulation or a combination of the two, but Eldrich started to change. He got stranger. Much stranger than his normal strange, which was pretty strange to begin with. He became obsessed with what he called the power of the "Alternaverse"—which was this new reality that we were supposed to embrace by doing things in a contrary or opposite fashion to the way in which they're normally done. It was a kind of a "free yourself by doing the unexpected" manifesto. Shout when you're supposed to be silent. Laugh at inappropriate moments. Get on a subway and sit right beside the only person on the car. Skip down the grocery-store aisle. Sing in elevators. That sort of thing. Eldrich said that God has a well-developed sense of humour, and that God is bored with our human habits and we need to be more amusing. He said we had to shake things up, to jolt ourselves out of our mind-and-soul-numbing routines.

This, of course, led to a lot of unpredictable and bizarre behaviour from both Eldrich and Seekers who were eager to demonstrate their acceptance and devotion. At times it was like living in some kind of loopy Monty Python sketch. You'd go into the kitchen and say good morning to someone, and they'd bark at you and do a somersault. Or you'd pour yourself a glass of juice and someone would grab it and dump it over their own head. Seriously.

You'd find people sleeping under the beds or on top of the piano. And all of Phil's stuff got moved around. Eldrich had Drew, Tyson and Wayne move everything into nonsensical arrangements—furnishings all pushed up in the middle of a room, lamps Krazy Glued to the ceilings. Expensive Persian rugs nailed to the walls. A madhouse.

And then, in addition to the whole Alternaverse thing, Eldrich became fixated on the number nine. Nine was this holy number and suddenly everything had to be done nine times or divided into nine pieces or have some relationship to nine. I didn't believe in the nine thing at all, but adherence to the concept was annoyingly contagious. I'd find myself stirring my coffee or twirling my spaghetti nine times, or jogging extra minutes on the treadmill so the digits would add up to nine. It was irritating.

Also irritating—and worrisome—was Eldrich's plan to start a magic mushroom farm in Phil's basement. Psilocybin is a Schedule III banned substance. I know because I took the time to Google it. I learned that if some disgruntled Seeker decided to rat us out, we'd be looking at a ten-year max prison sentence for "production." I warned Eldrich about it, but he didn't listen. And Phil wouldn't listen either. He trusted Eldrich, who insisted that mushrooms were part of the Institute's holy sacrament, and that if push came to shove, religious freedom would prevail over misguided, archaic drug laws. Yeah right. Tell it to the judges who had to enforce mandatory minimum sentences for drug offences. Did it matter that Mushroom Steve was inept and never managed to grow anything useful (his "crop" kept coming up mouldy and toxic)? No, it didn't. Because Steve never bothered to get rid of his equipment when he gave up his grow op. Did I ask him to carefully dispose of everything? Yes, of course. Did he tell me that he had done it? Oh yes, he assured me that he had. But what knuckle-nuts had actually done was stash three dozen Mason jars full of psilocybin spores behind Phil's furnace, which is where the police easily found them on the night of the raid. So fuck you very much, Steve, you idiot. As if my life wasn't difficult enough right now.

Anyway, back to Eldrich. It was around that time—Alternaverse, nine obsession, mushroom farm—that the touch therapy and the nonverbal thing started up, and soon after that all the sexual stuff.

Eldrich

$1 \times 9 = 9$
$2 \times 9 = 18: 1 + 8 = 9$
$3 \times 9 = 27: 2 + 7 = 9$
$4 \times 9 = 36: 3 + 6 = 9$
$5 \times 9 = 45: 4 + 5 = 9$
$6 \times 9 = 54: 5 + 4 = 9$
$7 \times 9 = 63: 6 + 3 = 9$
$8 \times 9 = 72: 7 + 2 = 9$
$9 \times 9 = 81: 8 + 1 = 9$
$10 \times 9 = 90: 9 + 0 = 9$
$11 \times 9 = 99: 9 + 9 = 18: 1 + 8 = 9$
$12 \times 9 = 108: 1 + 0 + 8 = 9$
$13 \times 9 = 117: 1 + 1 + 7 = 9$

Nine is Magic. The root of many mysteries. Our guiding numeral.

81 Elderbrook Avenue. $8 + 1 = 9$. Phil's age when we met: 54. $5 + 4 = 9$. Raine's age when we met: 45. $4 + 5 = 9$.

John

If I'm going to be entirely honest, it was one of the best summers of my life. Weird as hell, but fucking fun. I'll never have
another like it. So oddball. So vivid. A typical day: I awake in a
giant white bubble with an orange-haired beauty. We fuck. Or
we don't. Then off she trots to manage the Institute, while I
drift back to sleep or lounge long. Maybe a little radio or a hit
off a spliff before I amble through gardens lovely and fragrant
to the big house for coffee.

Along the way, I encounter several congregants practising what I assume to be Eldrich's prescribed "Alternaverse"
behaviours, i.e., free yourself/get closer to God by acting
like a deranged lunatic. I overtake sixty-something Moina,
crab-walking backwards across the lawn—her breasts hanging over her sides like eggs sliding off a plate. I pass a Speedo-
sporting teen, tenderly caressing the barbecue, murmuring to
it in Sinhalese, and out of the corner of my eye I spy Mindy,
urinating in a flower bed while singing "Return to Pooh
Corner" in a British-y accent.

Just another morning at 81 Elderbrook.

Dodging crazies in the kitchen, I make myself a cappuccino or a creamy, sweet latte, which I enjoy on the deck, usually

with some fresh fruit or Greek yogurt crowned with Heather's superb homemade granola (it has toasted sesame seeds and candied ginger). I hold the *Globe and Mail* high to keep Seekers at bay until I'm ready for contact (always post-caffeine).

After brekkie, I check in with the boss lady. I find Amy and minions processing and packaging up website sale items, preparing for Drew's daily drive to the post office. Oddly, the factory-like efficiency of this endeavour perturbs me more than any Alternaverse freakiness—all those eight-by-ten glossies of Eldrich, looking dreamy and wise, spread out across the floor, ready to be slipped into envelopes and mailed to maniacs across North America. I sign anything that needs to be signed, and maybe monitor some site stats (inevitably surprising; we grow stupidly rich) before skedaddling. Then a quick howdy to Eldrich, who's composing his daily tweet, or leading the flock through some quiet yoga or tai chi, or, if Phil's awake (unlikely at this point, since he sleeps sixteen hours a night while his body repairs), a drumming circle or an interpretive dance, or one of his Alternaverse exercises, like playing Satie on Phil's baby grand with his nose. I wave bye-bye and head for a jog through the 'hood or a ride through Wilket Creek Park. Phil, of course, has a fine collection of bicycles, most of which have been custom designed and are therefore too small for me. But there's one, a Jerónimo Slütter Ti XCross, all titanium and amber leather, that must have belonged to his hubby and is just big enough. Comfortable and stylin'. After a hot, sweaty, endorphin-inducing workout, I strip down and plunge into the cool of the pool. Bliss. Then I sun-dry like a lizard on a rock, or merely towel off, before striding to the big house for lunch.

My mid-afternoon repast usually consists of a variety of cold salads, a sandwich and a bar of chocolate. After which I return to my bubble with the familiar, delicious throb that is the desire to work. I throw the iPod on shuffle and make MAMA for as long as I like, generally unmolested, unless Amy tries to persuade me to attend a meeting, or Eldrich tries to drag me along on one of his ruminating rambles through the Wilket woods. Then, when I'm fatigued or no longer feeling it, I go in search of my patron.

I make it a point every day to have a tête-a-tête with Phil. It's important that he knows who his real friends are. And frankly, I enjoy it. I mix myself a cocktail and blend him a daily healthful smoothie made with apple chunks, an entire Meyer lemon, blueberries, red grapefruit, probiotic yogurt, turmeric, flaxseed and pomegranate juice. Then we sit and sip our respective beverages in the garden or, if he's too tired to move around, in his bed. Sometimes we watch *Storage Wars*. We just adore *Storage Wars*. I love Barry, and Phil loves Jarrod and Brandi.

After our confab, I go and answer site correspondence on my shiny new iPad (thanks, Institute), a tiresome task, but Amy insists that I pull at least a percentage of my weight. She eventually finds me and we discuss our respective days (at 81 Elderbrook, there's always something amusing to share) and debate our dining options—i.e., should we chow down with the clan or hightail it to a restaurant near or far. At that time of the day, there's usually some communal barbecue action going on—Mushroom Steve is a surprisingly good cook—and it's easy to saunter over and pluck a burger, sausage or cob of corn off the grill, which is what we do almost every evening. There's really no reason to leave. After dinner and some conversing with the congregants, we go over any business matters that need to be tended to on the morrow—payroll, supplies, accounts receivable, etc. Not that I understand or give a rat's nut sack about any of it, I just want my gal-pal to think I'm keeping tabs on the till. When that's done, we kick back and watch some TV or a flick in the basement theatre, or go for a swim or a hot tub, or retire to the bubble to smoke pot and fool around or just read and surf the Net.

Pretty fucking sweet. Talk about an Alternaverse.

If only it could have lasted . . .

Of course, the living wasn't *all* easy all summer. If Raine happened to descend, which was more and more often as the season wound down, Amy instantly became satellite, faithfully orbiting the dwarf star. She'd claim she was merely tending to a "high-profile donor" (and I was being "possessive and weird" if I questioned her about it), but her attentions seemed to extend beyond playing the good host. A good host, for example, doesn't have to suddenly go for pedicures or purchase an eyelash curler and spend an extra half-hour getting ready every morning. A good host can smile and nod politely, and doesn't need to bray like a coked-up donkey every time a high-profile donor makes a heroic but ultimately unsuccessful attempt at a witticism. No. It was obvious to me that Amy was in a bit of a Maddox tizzy. And she wasn't the only one. Eldrich, who I had pegged as asexual, or possibly gay and closeted, sprang fully, sexually to life as soon as Raine showed up with his daughter, Coco, in tow. Lovely Coco, with her soft blond curls, snub nose and wide blue eyes. Curvy Coco with her titties up high and her Bubblicious behind. Fourteen-year-old Coco with her adorable shaved pussy—I know because of the scanty crocheted bikini she favoured. The girl gave every straight man at Elderbrook a relentless hard-on (I'll probably be jerking off to her twenty years from now), but most of them knew not to mess with our star-congregant's wittle baby-doll.

Most of them, but much to my astonishment (and amusement), not all of them.

Nope.

Amy

The meetings changed. For the longest time they followed the same format. Eldrich would discuss one spiritual topic or another, maybe read from a text or his notebook, and then take questions or have dialogues with congregants. Then one day, something different. As usual, he was there before anyone else, seated cross-legged on the stage, waiting for Seekers to arrive and settle. But on this particular day he didn't start to talk when everyone was quiet. On this day he just sat there, slowly shifting his gaze from this person to that as the tension in the room mounted. *What was going on? When would he begin? Why wasn't he speaking?*

Confusion and discomfort grew increasingly palpable as congregants checked each other for reactions, nobody daring to question the silence or the spell he was silently casting. There were nervous giggles, coughs and throat clearings before a calm gradually began to spread in an invisible wave. You could feel that too. A sort of smoothing, a relaxing. Like a Doberman that'd been on high alert lying down and closing its eyes.

Once tranquility had suffused the room—about fifteen to twenty minutes into the gathering—Eldrich fixed his eyes on

Marina and kept them there. He had a tiny smile on his face. A kind and affectionate smile. Marina stared back. A minute passed, maybe a bit more or less. Then, out of nowhere, she exploded into tears and proceeded to sob mightily, as if every ounce of pain were being wrung from her soul. Eldrich watched for a moment, then went to her and embraced her. She wailed even harder in his arms—anguished animal howls, her body shaking and shaking. And then, little by little, the quaking subsided and the sobs became whimpers and then deep sighs, and finally slow regular breaths, which is when he released her. She blew her nose and dried her eyes. She smiled. No, she *beamed*. I'd never seen her look so happy, or happy at all, for that matter. Marina was not a happy human. There seemed to be an ocean of sadness sloshing behind her blank, ashen facade. But right then in that moment she looked truly joyful. She had colour in her cheeks. She looked . . . shiny. Everyone applauded as she grabbed Eldrich's hands and kissed and kissed them.

Seekers were crying and laughing and cheering.

Group catharsis.

I personally found it to be an extremely moving and powerful display. Somehow, wordlessly, Eldrich had provided a spiritual cleansing, one that seemed to offer profound relief. Everyone who witnessed it wanted to experience it for themselves.

And from then on, that's how the meetings went. It became a huge draw. A kind of premium experience that everybody wanted to try. Seekers sometimes spoke, but Eldrich never did. He would begin onstage, randomly scanning the crowd.

Eventually, his eyes would linger and then lock on somebody. A silent communication would ensue. Sometimes the person would sit quietly and drink it in, bask in it. More often, the person would erupt into a crying jag, or laugh uproariously, or shout praise to God. Some even spoke in tongues, writhed crazily on the floor or fainted dead away. The effect was always sizable, and the staring session always ended with Eldrich coming over to touch and calm the individual. Touch was a big part of it. It could be a tight embrace, or a kiss held firmly on the forehead or eyelids, or a hand pressed over the heart. It changed depending on who was on the receiving end. And over time, the touching became less controlled, more impulsive, almost . . . feral. But always very compassionate and loving. Like a lion with a cub, there was a lot of nuzzling, some gentle biting, even some licking. I know it sounds strange, but it was actually quite lovely: primal and protective and natural.

Oddly enough, the meetings in which Seekers could converse with Eldrich about their lives and spiritual questions were not nearly as popular as the ones in which Eldrich said nothing at all.

Eldrich

Words, words, words, words, words, words, words. Behind words: meaning. Beyond meaning: truth. Mathematical, molecular truth.

Touch is truth.

We are made of each other. We are made of the cosmos. Carbon, nitrogen, oxygen. All of us, atoms. All of us, atomically connected. We came from the universe and we will return to the universe. We will not cease to be.

Our bodies die, but our atoms, which came from stars, are eternal. They will go on to become parts of other matter and other humans. Shakespeare's atoms are in me. Gandhi's atoms are in you. Someday you will be in me, and I will be in you.

Reincarnation. Re-embodiment.

Life everlasting.

We can never die. We are infinitely and mysteriously transforming.

Changing.

John

What a genius freak our boy Eldrich was. He figured out a way—all in the name of enlightenment, of course—to work less, earn more *and* get his hungry hands on Coco without getting daddy's back up (initially, anyway). Bravo! A triumph! A guru tour de force!

Want to know how he did it? By shutting his trap.

I first heard about it from Amy but didn't pay any attention. I'd begged off attending most meetings and seminars and was focused on building MAMA. My preliminary construction plan hadn't been working to my satisfaction, so I decided to embark on a far more ambitious interpretation than what I'd imagined in the beginning. Inspired by Ron Mueck's sixteen-foot newborn in the National Gallery, I chose to construct a hyper-real MAMA from fibreglass and silicone. I knew basically how to do it. Years ago, I had a fling with an artist who created prosthetics for film and TV. I helped her make dozens of aliens when she was scrambling to meet a deadline. It was very cool and fun. Expensive as hell, but since money was coming in on a regular basis, I figured I could swing it with MAMA. I decided to buy a new womb too. I'd ditched my first attempt at constructing one—a kind of oversized, cashew-shaped doggy bed that I'd stuffed with memory foam and lined with soft fleece dyed pink. It looked OK and felt nice, but it was just too flaccid. Too flat. It didn't *surround* properly. I scrapped it when I stumbled upon the idea of stereo chair as uterus. They were big in the 1960s. Egg-shaped. Very mod. Also comfy and encompassing. Plus they had built-in speakers. You could find retro ones for sale on eBay. But here's the best part: there was a company in Fairfield, New Jersey, selling glossy new ones with high-quality sound systems that could hook up to your iPad/iPod. Perfect. I could lay one on its side and secure it, and it would have just the right heft and structure for my crawl-in womb. Cozy too. All of this is a long way of saying that as soon as my cardinal-red, deluxe modPod egg chair arrived at Elderbrook, I became entirely engrossed in MAMA and stopped attending meetings altogether. That is, until Amy forced me to check out Eldrich's new act (*You can't just hide in your bubble all the time!*).

Here's how it worked: he showed up and did fuck all. Nada. Bupkis. He'd sit his ass down on stage and look at people. That's it. That's what the throngs were lining up to shell out for. That's what everyone was so excited about. Eldrich just sitting there. Looking. When half an hour had elapsed or when whomever he was staring at started to blubber or lapse into some theatrical grand mal–type seizure, he'd amble over and swathe them in his gangly, giant self, pet and coddle for a while—hug, kiss, stroke, cocoon—until they were all spent and calm and grateful, positively glowing with worship. And that was that.

I'm not kidding.

And the people were loving it, slurping it up with great big hungry spoons.

The day I attended, Eldrich decided to fix his sights on young Coco (surprise, surprise), who was making her second visit with daddy-o. Our boy stared and stared (managing somehow to keep his gaze from drifting down from her rapt, wide-set eyes to her rapt, wide-set breasts, charmingly discernible through a faux-distressed, LA-designer T-shirt), and as soon as the girl's baby blues grew the tiniest bit moist (it could have been allergies), he went for her, pouncing, enfolding, fondling, nosing . . . It continued on for a disturbingly long time. He was even licking her head at one point, mere feet from Raine, who looked on smilingly, approvingly. A real proud papa.

Go figure.

Unfortunately, Eldrich's shut-up-and-grope routine proved a bit too inspiring for the masses. The serene, blissed-out devotion of Seekers—a state I was accustomed to and comfortable with—began to morph into a kind of rapturous hysteria. More and more fervent types were showing up, eager to get to Eldrich and his ostensibly curative orbs. Rumour was his "God Gaze" could heal everything from PTSD to vaginal warts (I thought: *Call me when he can cook up some Superfries with them peepers*).

Mushroom Steve went from being faithful sidekick to awestruck humble servant. He began to shadow Eldrich constantly, and grew creepily protective of his master—personally doing all his laundry by hand, preparing special meals and carrying them to the bedroom, where Eldrich had taken to hiding out for long stretches of time. He also enlisted Tyson and Wayne to act as sentries, guarding the door to keep

Seekers at bay. Even *I* was denied access when I wanted a word one morning. An unnerving turn of events. Steve poked his head out the door and whispered that Eldrich was meditating, but if I had something "essential" to discuss, I could try again after lunch. Then he asked if he could speak to me about something.

He led me down the hall and, all smiles and munificence, said he wanted to "commission" me to do a bust of Eldrich. In bronze. I laughed in his face, thinking he was having me on. Nope. His alarmingly dilated pupils were brimming with sincerity (like one of those big-eyed velvet-painting tykes).

"Does Eldrich know about this?" I asked.

"No. No way, man! Eldrich is, like, the most humble dude in the world! You know that. He's like, crazy humble. But that doesn't mean *we* can't honour him, right?"

Wrong. I disrespectfully declined—told him I'd love to help out but was too busy working on my bust of Kim Jong-un. He was not amused.

Amy, who was well aware of the rising Eldrich frenzy, had done nothing to quell the swell of screaming meemies. On the contrary (without consulting me), she went ahead and plastered the website with zealous testimonials, superimposed over a full-screen close-up of Eldrich staring intensely out at the viewer. *"You* have *to experience it! His force emanates across the room and fills you with luminous self-knowledge."* / *"I felt potent waves of spiritual influence penetrating my soul."* / *"He preaches silently, but you hear it louder than any voice!"* / *"It was like he was channelling the Lord's grace through his gaze, I felt years of pain being replaced with blissful effulgence."* Um . . . OK. I had to look up "effulgence," which sounds like something that spews from the sewer but in fact means radiant splendour.

Radiant splendour, Amy decided, doesn't come cheap. She doubled the price of weekend meetings to eighty bucks a pop for first-timers, and forty for repeat visitors.

Ordinarily this wouldn't have bothered me. If it were all knitting-store proprietors and documentary filmmakers with digs in the Annex shelling out for illumination, tantric-y Os or huggy-wugs, I would have been delighted. But when I saw someone I recognized—a dude who lived on a sewer grate at Simcoe and Dundas, and carved bars of soap into figurines to sell for spare change—when I saw that dude limp in with scabby, frostbitten fists full of rolled-up coins, looking to have his multiple sclerosis healed, I figured things were getting out of control. And later that day when I spied a young woman snailing frailly up Elderbrook Avenue, wheeling her oxygen tank along the icy sidewalk, I knew I had to act.

I went in search of Amy and was told she was by the snack bar in the basement (or what used to be the snack bar—Amy, Drew and Anne-Marie's son, Richard, had recently transformed the area into a makeshift gift shop). I found her and Drew seated at a table, chiselling chunks of purple stone into tiny fragments.

"What's up?" I said, perplexed by the geological activity.

"Hey. We're just getting these ready for Eldrich," said Amy.

"To bless," said Drew, reading my confusion.

Turns out these two had concocted a scheme to purchase Auralite crystals in bulk from a mine in Aurora, then unload them (at a 500 percent markup) after Eldrich had "blessed"

them, i.e., ramped up their already stupendous healing powers by snoozing with them under his pillow, or carrying them
around in his enchanted pockets.

"What a magical idea," I said, causing Drew's pimply cheeks
to flush with pride. "Mind if I borrow the boss lady for a bit?"

"Be my guest," said Drew, perfectly happy to tap away
alone, like a little elf with his wee hammer.

I dragged Amy to the bubble, where I grilled her about
all the commotion and cash grabs of late. She instantly went
on the offensive (as usual), accusing me of being totally out
of touch with what was going on at the Institute, of grossly
misinterpreting her actions and egregiously misunderstanding
her intentions. She wasn't being avaricious. Not at all. She just
felt bad for Phil because so many new Seekers were suddenly
flocking to his property. She was just trying to get us into a
new headquarters and out of Phil's hair as quickly as possible.
And given the current real estate market, that, unfortunately,
required a whack of dough.

Plausible (as usual), maddeningly so. Amy assured me she
wasn't being greedy, she was being thoughtful. And how could
I not know that? How insulting. Furthermore, I had zero right
to criticize how she was running the Institute, since I was forever disappearing into my bubble to work on MAMA. She recommended I step up and get more involved if I had a problem
with how things were going. Or, conversely, if I was uncomfortable with how things were going and didn't want to get
involved to change those things, I was certainly free to get the
hell out.

Am-scray. Vamoose.

I ended up apologizing (as usual). Then we had hot makeup sex (also, as usual). It was confusing. Afterward, we lay in the early evening darkness and listened to freezing rain *ping* off the bubble roof. Amy whispered that the Institute would never turn away a Seeker in need, whether that person had money or not. Never *ever*. But she felt it was important to keep prices high for those who could afford it—*for Phil's sake*. I didn't argue.

The following morning, Amy handed me an Institute cheque to cover the cost of my modPod egg chair. She said it made sense for the Institute to contribute, since Seekers would undoubtedly want to experience MAMA once she was done. She called it a legitimate "supply."

I took the cheque, wondering why, if she was so desperate to accumulate cash "for Phil's sake," this was suddenly a priority. But I didn't say anything. I just folded it into my wallet.

Later, I left the compound to try to clear my head. I went downtown and wandered through Kensington Market (you know you're living with weirdos when the denizens of that district seem normal by comparison). I bought a few Christmas gifts for Amy, then hit the AGO to check out the Frida and Diego exhibit. It was great. And just great to be out, looking at art. Back in the day, everyone thought Rivera was the thing. He got far more attention than his unibrowed gal-pal. But Frida was clearly the superior artist. It was so obvious now. I lingered long, then grabbed some takeout from Asian Legend and cabbed up to Hawton Boulevard to chow down and hang in the old digs. I figured I'd have lunch and then maybe a nap or a wank.

Consider my surprise when I entered the living room and discovered a spanking-new sectional sofa, groovy shag rug and sixty-inch wall-mounted HDTV. Amy's thirty-two incher had been relegated to her bedroom. In her closet: a bunch of duds I'd never seen before, including a half-dozen cashmere cardigans in a rainbow of pastel shades, a buttery leather jacket and a row of designer shoes, most of them still bearing their ludicrously high price tags.

Who knew she had even been coming here?

Had she used her salary to purchase these items? Possibly. She was certainly paying herself enough. Or were those five pair of Fiorentini and Baker boots also Institute "supplies"?

Could I even ask her that question? Certainly not without inciting another mammoth fight. And probably not at all, not anymore, since I had already deposited my twenty-three-hundred-dollar modPod egg chair cheque.

Hmm.

I reclined on the chaise lounge portion of the sofa (so comfy), switched on the giant TV (such wonderful brightness and contrast) and tucked into my Asian Legend (damned delicious). But in truth, I was feeling distracted. Dyspeptic. I couldn't stop thinking about sewer-grate man and oxygen girl, and wondering if my Adam was on his way to becoming a fallen angel.

Amy

If I knew then what I know now about John's background, I might not have been so offended by his suspicious mind. But since he never opened up to me, I had no idea why he was always so mistrustful and accusatory. I couldn't understand why he kept pointing the finger at what he imagined to be my bad and dodgy behaviour.

It seemed very unfair.

There I was, working my ass off, basically running the Institute on my own so that John was free to be the artist I believed him to be. I was trying to help emotionally and physically fragile Seekers find solace and inspiration with Eldrich, and doing my best to help Phil get his home and health back, but all I got from John was distrust, skepticism and repeated unwarranted attacks on my character.

It was more than unfair. It was hurtful.

John seemed determined to push me away, when all I ever wanted was to connect and get close.

ATTENTION SEEKERS

Due to overwhelming demand, Eldrich will no longer be holding open Blends™ in the pool. If you would like to join in, please use the sheet below to sign up for tomorrow's Blend™, which will take place at 9 a.m. sharp. Please note: this will be a silent Blend™ and Eldrich cannot answer any direct questions. If you wish to commune verbally with Eldrich, please see me to book a session. (Note: We are already booking well into the New Year.) Thank you for your understanding, cooperation and trueness.

Peace and warm puppies,
Steve

GROUP 1	GROUP 2	GROUP 3
1. Steve	1. Perry	1. Joyanne
2. Drew	2. Moina	2. Randall
3. Catelyn	3. Heather	3. Marina
4. Wayne	4. Sanjeev	4. Richard
5. Tyson	5. Danny	5. Jeff
6. Anne-Marie	6. Jane	6. Holly
7. Robyn	7. Masako	7. Sue B.
8. Mindy	8. Christine	8. Conan
9. Alexa	9. Phil	9. Jason

John

Human Jenga on the family-room floor. Olive-oil Twister in the kitchen. Twice daily "Blends," i.e., synchronized group gropes in the swimming pool . . . Touch was the new Talk at the Institute.

I saw it everywhere around the compound, Seekers glued to each other in small or large clusters, coiled on couches, bobbing in the hot tub, mouthing one another, rubbing.

Did I partake? No, I did not. Even though there were at least half a dozen objectively appetizing females gamboling about Phil's pretty much all the time and especially on weekends, I had nearly zero inclination to handle them. When the ubiquitous canoodling and so-called "therapeutic touch" sessions naturally (inevitably) morphed into Institute-sanctioned fuck fests, I still kept mine in my pants. Why? Because these people were crackers. Banana-fruity-flavours. Seriously, sadly, irreparably damaged goods. Likely crawling with STDs to boot. I had no intention of swapping fluids with them.

Besides, I had Amy, my loving and devoted partner.

Amy

I am not a prude. Unlike some. If consenting adult Seekers wanted to engage in therapeutic touch or remedial sexual activities, whether in pairs or larger groups, I wasn't going to judge them. In fact, I found the physical/nonverbal conduct a lot easier to live with than all the Alternaverse weirdness that had been going on through the summer and fall.

Touch is medicinal. People need it. We really do require contact. This is not my opinion. This is a fact. Think of Harlow and his famous experiment with rhesus monkeys. I learned about it in first-year psych. What happened was infant monkeys were taken from their mothers a couple of hours after birth. They were given two surrogate mothers instead. The first was a wire mother, cold and unyielding, which provided what was then considered all-important: food. The second was a terrycloth mother, soft and comfortable, which gave no food at all. Guess which one the babies gravitated to and spent almost all of their time with? The cloth mothers. Touch was even more important than nursing/sustenance. Touch *was* sustenance.

Touch became a major part of Eldrich's philosophy of spiritual connection and healing. Seekers were benefiting from it. I saw it with my own eyes. People were happier. Calmer. More hopeful and content. A lot of bad energy was being smoothed away. It worked, so it lasted, unlike the Alternaverse madness, which had largely faded into the background.

So you tell me, was it so horribly wrong to respond when someone reached out and asked me to participate in a Blend? Am I a wicked, evil person who needs to be endlessly disparaged because I decided to try what everyone else seemed to be learning and gaining from? Should I be condemned and punished because I shared an innocent and affectionate embrace on one occasion with someone I felt an immediate kinship with?

I don't think so. But that's just me.

John

I heard them long before I saw them.

It was Christmas Eve. And far too many creatures were stirring at Elderbrook. You'd think that Seekers would have left to be with family that night. Wrong. It seems we *were* family.

There was abundant cooking, feasting, drinking and merry-making (Heather was baking up a storm in the kitchen) but nothing official. No meetings scheduled. And only a coterie of core faithful allowed on-site. Except for one. A special guest. Dr. Peter Scheibling—a strapping young ethnobotanist from Albuquerque. Raine had recruited him in his efforts to begin holding regular ayahuasca ceremonies at Phil's place. Peter wanted to check out the joint, get the lay of the land and see if it was worth the risk bringing the drugs (he called it "medicine") into Canada and administering them. Scheibling had visited Peru and Brazil many times and had studied extensively with various shamans. He claimed to know what he was doing, how to concoct and serve the brew, what kind of diet to follow in preparation, what drug interactions to look out for. He told us he used to belong to a church in Santa Cruz that used ayahuasca in its services. According to him, there were ayahuasca ceremonies being held regularly all over North America. You just had to know where to find them. He said he'd heard about a Toronto doctor who was quietly experimenting with ayahuasca as a cure for drug addiction, and that he would try to track her down to see if he could tap into her supply. He seemed friendly, bright and knowledgeable, but for a scientist, awfully airy-fairy. He had long blond hair that rippled down to his waist, a studded eyebrow and two strangely pierced ears—the stretched-out kind with gaping holes in the lobes that you could poke your finger through. And although he arrived in normal clothing, he immediately went to the guest room and changed into a kind of Moroccan dress for men (it looked like pyjamas) with a pair of Uggs and an earflap hat. Somehow, he carried it off, still looked masculine. He smelled strongly of cinnamon oil.

People were drawn to him. Maybe because Raine presented him as if he were some illustrious dignitary who had deigned to grace us with a visit. Phil thought he was hunky (*Oh my God, it's Fabio!*) and got all giggly around him. Eldrich and Steve were clearly enamoured, listening raptly to his Amazonian adventure anecdotes, hanging on his every word as if he himself were a shaman. Young Coco, who seemed to know him fairly well, was inordinately playful and flirty, plucking his hat from his head and trying it on, offering to braid his hair, fingering his leather bracelet (all of this driving Eldrich quietly mad, which was fun to observe).

After dinner, Peter held court before the fireplace in the formal living room. I stuck around for a while, but when Peter, Eldrich and Steve went off to do "research" (i.e., mushrooms) and Phil went to bed, I headed back to my bubble. I was one of the chosen few invited to participate, but I wasn't in the mood. Amy was at her parents' place for the evening, so I had a chance to get some work done before she got home. And I was on an interesting part. The audio. I had completed the major casting and most of the detail finishes on MAMA. Now I just had to add the door on the womb and the giant eyeballs, which my friend Jocelyn was making out of glass (remaking, actually; I wasn't happy with the first pair). It was a ton of fun mixing and fiddling with the sounds I'd recorded and downloaded. Catelyn had graciously provided the sweet murmurings of MAMA. She wasn't a big girl, but she had a lovely low voice. Very mellifluous. I just needed to blend the right amount of reverbed heartbeat and womb *whoosh*, and then figure out optimal repetition interludes. So that's what I was playing with until about 11:30 or so, when I decided to brave the cold and go nab some of the treats Heather and Staci had been baking all evening.

The house was strangely peaceful, the kitchen empty and lovely—illuminated only by stove light, the throaty *whir* of the dishwasher churning, the aroma of lemon loaf and butter tarts cooling on the counter. It was cozy and Christmasy, and it made me feel oddly happy. But where was everyone?

I poked my head into the den and saw Tyson and Wayne playing a silent, brooding game of chess in front of the fire. In the basement theatre, a handful of Seekers were watching *It's a Wonderful Life*—Alexa, Mindy, Anne-Marie and her son, Moina and Perry, holding hands, weeping. No sign of the mushroom trio, though. They must have holed up in one of the bedrooms. I opted not to seek them out, grabbed some baked goods and, feeling strangely elated, headed back to my bubble. As I was sprinting across the lawn I heard something—something besides the icy grass crunching under my sneakers. A familiar sound. A familiar Amy sound.

It was coming from the pool.

As I moved toward it, the sound grew more intense and then disappeared.

The pool lights were off, and all I could see was a thick mass of steam rising from the balmy water. It looked sinister, like a great boiling witches' brew in some hellish cauldron. It was only when I was right at the pool's edge that I spotted them. She was clinging to him in the shallow end. Her arms around his neck, her legs wrapped tightly around his hips. They weren't moving.

I wish I had said something snappy, but a tsunami of epinephrine was sloshing over my brain, short-circuiting the synapses. *"What the fuck!"*

"Oh!" said Amy, releasing, pushing away.

Since then, so many rejoinders, but at the time . . . nada.

"Johnny!" said Raine, with a big stupid smile on his face. "Come on in, the water's fine!" He stood and opened his personally-trained arms wide, gesturing for me to join them.

I winged a butter tart at his head. It hit hard and exploded off his left temple.

"Hey!" screamed Amy.

I fired another one that thudded against his chest.

"Not cool!" shouted Raine. But I didn't respond, I was out of there.

Soon after, they showed up at the bubble, all earnest and mature and soft-spoken, determined to talk me down, trying to tell me that they were just practising the Institute's touch therapy, and that what had happened between them in the pool was nothing more than an innocent and godly interaction, and how could I be so possessive and ridiculous and angry?

I was pretty composed by then (after smoking a j and swallowing a massive quantity of whiskey); the river wasn't calm, but it had frozen over. I listened quietly with a mild-mannered smile on my face. I sipped the prosecco they had brought along. I nodded and nodded in apparent understanding.

"Look, man," said Raine, slapping my knee. "I know you and Amy are together! Everyone knows that. And I have a lady friend back in New York!"

Nod. Sip.

"Amy and I were just connecting in the Lord's love. Nothing smarmy about that. That's a beautiful thing to do, right? That's why I invited you to join us!"

Sip. Nod.

"You should have," said Amy.

"Seriously man, would I have invited you to join us if we were tryin' to hide somethin'? I mean, think about it."

I considered. I nodded. "OK," I said.

They were pretty convincing, actually. Maybe Raine wasn't such a shitty actor after all. I may have even believed them if I hadn't heard that sound. That familiar Amy sound.

It was the sound she makes when you fill her with cum.

"So we're good?" said Raine, squeezing my knee and rising.

"Yeah, we're good."

"All right," he said. "I'll see you guys in the morning. Merry Christmas!"

"Merry Christmas," said Amy with a little wave.

But we didn't see him in the morning. I'm happy to report that I never saw the large-headed, thick-thighed dipshit again. Because he left Elderbrook that very night. He left soon after returning to the house and discovering that young Coco was not sleeping peacefully in the guest room like she was supposed to be. No. According to Amy, Raine found darling Coco in Eldrich and Steve's room, starkers with her mouth full of Peter Scheibling's balls and her legs spread wide as Eldrich attempted to cram his colossal schlong into her teeny tween twat (while Steve-o knelt behind him, tonguing his master's glory hole and jerking himself off).

It seems the mushroom trio had gone cuckoo for Coco puffs.

My absolute fave part was that degenerate-Eldrich and his pervy crew reportedly gave Raine the same spiritual-connection spiel that he and Amy had laid on me in the bubble.

When I heard that, I remember thinking: *Maybe there is a God. And maybe Eldrich is right about his magnificent sense of humour.*

Eldrich

Things fall apart. The centre cannot hold.

Emotions flare. Emotions obscure.

Raine's last visit with us was at Christmas. John moved back to Hawton Boulevard in January. But neither of them ever denounced the Institute. Not once. Not ever.

Whoever suggests such a thing is a liar.

Amy

So . . . Eldrich, soaring on psilocybin and suffering a horrendous lapse of judgment, tried (and thankfully failed) to have unprotected intercourse with Raine's fourteen-year-old daughter. Unfortunately, Mushroom Steve and Peter Scheibling were in on it too. A group thing. Not at all unusual for the Institute at that point, except for the underage-minor portion of the equation. Was the girl sexually compromised? Yes, of course. Three adult males took her to bed—though not against her will at least. Coco admitted that she'd sought out the men and initiated the escapade. But who knows how far she meant it to go. Did she leave the Institute as a virgin? Yes, assuming she arrived as one. There was nudity and oral, but no actual penetration.

Thank heaven for small mercies and huge cocks.

Raine, who stumbled upon them in flagrante delicto, was, I thought, incredibly reasonable about the whole thing. Of course, he took his kid and split right aw   -w didn't even have a chance to say goodbye—and he   ediately severed official ties to the Institute (he texted   airport, asking me to remove his endorsement   om the website, which I had Wayne do right after   ut he didn't press charges and he never spoke out about what had happened. Even after everything went horribly wrong, when reporters were all over Raine, digging for dirt, clamouring to know why he had dissociated himself from the Institute (no more tweets/visits), he remained astonishingly tight-lipped and restrained, stating that while he felt that the Institute had done a lot of fine work, and that Eldrich had a good heart and a lot of positive views on how to live a life rich in God, he couldn't get behind *all* of the Institute's philosophies and so had decided to pursue his own spiritual path.

Amazing.

You know, John loves to slag Raine, but not only did the man not rat us out (and capitalize on an opportunity for endless publicity), he was also incredibly supportive and gracious when we needed him to be. I mean, we're already in legal hell; the last thing we need is a statutory rape indictment on top of everything else. I think we should be very grateful for Raine's loyalty and wisdom. Unlike your typical person, he was able to see past his own emotional response. He was able to detach from assumptions and try to really *understand* what had happened. He knew that one slip-up of judgment didn't define Eldrich or the Institute. Give the man some respect.

Anyway . . . as everyone already knows, things went sideways after Christmas. John dumped me and pretty much took off as soon as his sculpture was finished. He would stop by to pick up his paycheque and cozy up to Phil. That was about it. He didn't do any work. Raine was out of the picture, of course. And I re   his energy and the excitement he generated on hi   Scheibling had settled in and,

together with Steve, was planning the big ayahuasca ceremony. The first thing he did was go through the kitchen and
get rid of anything that tasted remotely good. He put us on
the most bland and punishing diet for weeks. No sugar, salt,
oils, pork, fat, spices, bananas or apples. No alcohol. Nothing
processed, smoked or pickled. Nothing fermented or canned.
And worst of all, no caffeine! I spent the first two days in bed
with the world's worst migraine and boils sprouting on my
neck. Seriously, I had pus-oozing withdrawal pimples. It was
hideous. And that was followed by three weeks of mashed len-
tils and herbal tea. I lost nine pounds. He also banned sex and
masturbation, which made the men all testosteroney and hos-
tile. Plus the weather was unrelentingly awful. Freezing cold
and tons of snow. I felt trapped and depleted. It was the first
truly joyless period of the Institute. Everything had gone dark,
and things seemed to be getting worse and worse all the time.

I should have guessed something bad was coming.

As for the night of the ceremony . . . I'm not supposed to
talk about it.

And I don't want to talk about it.

~

Griffin

Holy Oliver Sacks, Batman! Drew Woollings has awakened! He focused his peepers. He spoke semi-coherently. He attempted a feeble squeeze of the damp mitt of Mama Bear, who managed, in her excitement, to unwedge herself from a hospital armchair (I usually had to hoist her out, and was thinking of installing a winch).

Guess what did it? A sleeping pill. Yes, that's right, a drug designed to induce somnolence. A little tab of zolpidem, otherwise known as Ambien—a pharmaceutical so mysterious and daffy not only does it sometimes cause sleep-walking, sleep-driving, sleep-bingeing and sleep-fucking, it can also rouse patients who have been in a persistent vegetative state for years. This was discovered by accident and relatively recently, so there haven't been a lot of clinical trials, but anecdotally it works in about 10 percent of patients. And it worked on our boy Drew! I was there when it first happened. A nurse administered the drug. Half an hour later, Drew's cheeks flushed with colour and he began making mumbly-grumbly sounds. The doctor was summoned. Soon after, Drew turned his head, looked at Doreen, who was already hyperventilating, and said, "Mommy?" She fountained into tears and lunged at her boy. A flurry of *I love yous* and *I love you toos* and *kissy-kissy* and *Am I in hospital?* and *Are you in pain?* and then all of it interrupted by the neurologist and his questions, so my only interaction was a sheepish wave when Doreen exclaimed, "Your best friend is here!" Drew was understandably confused. Mama chalked it up to the coma and I was off the hook. An hour later, Drew slipped back into unconsciousness, but the doctor assured Doreen that he would come around each time he took the drug, and that the neural pathways, thus stimulated, may well begin to heal.

Doreen would likely get her son back.

And I would likely get my story.

I took her to the Ikea cafeteria to celebrate.

PART III

PART III

Questioning the Answer Institute

They came from across Canada and the US, seeking spiritual
guidance and fulfillment. What they found was a New Age sect
that took their money, fed them hallucinogens and, for a core
group of devotees, cost them their lives.

AN EXCLUSIVE INSIDER'S TALE OF SEX, DRUGS AND AN ACT OF
GOD IN ONE OF TORONTO'S TONIEST NEIGHBOURHOODS

by Griffin Hill

IT DOESN'T LOOK LIKE A CHURCH.

In fact, 81 Elderbrook Avenue is a private residence in
Toronto's exclusive Bridle Path neighbourhood. The home was
purchased in 2010 by Chen Xi Quan—also known as "Phil"—a
Singaporean expat from one of that country's most powerful and
affluent families. Between November 2011 and February 2013,
Quan allowed his home to serve as headquarters for the Answer
Institute—a New Age, quasi-religious organization that promised
"enlightenment, healing and truth" to its followers. Today, the
luxurious house sits empty, cordoned off by police tape, pending
a criminal investigation into the deaths of nine Institute members—including Quan—and a legal battle contesting ownership of
the property.

Davinder and Bebe Dhaliwal have lived across the street from
81 Elderbrook for more than two decades. Like most houses in the
neighbourhood, theirs is set well back from the street and shielded

by trees and shrubbery. The Dhaliwals, both retired, are private people who have never kept tabs on their neighbours. Still, about a year ago, they started to notice a lot of cars parked up and down Elderbrook every weekend. "We assumed they were young people having parties," Davinder told me. "Sometimes we'd hear music or drumming, but it never went late and we were never disturbed, so we didn't pay much attention." It wasn't until the Dhaliwals were awakened by police and ambulance sirens in the early-morning hours of February 2 that they realized something more sinister might be going on across the street. And when they learned there had been ritualistic drug ceremonies and orgies taking place so close to their home, they were shocked. "We had no idea," Bebe says. "If we knew what was going on over there, we would have moved."

The figure at the centre of the Answer Institute, its spiritual leader, is Eldrich Becker, a self-described "metaphysician." He is tall and lanky, with shoulder-length brown hair, intense green eyes and a wide smile. He sports a three-day growth of facial hair, a loose-fitting white shirt, linen pants and worn-out Birkenstock sandals. There is something vaguely Christ-like about his appearance—the kind of modernized depiction you might find on a religious souvenir in a dollar store. His slow, soft way of speaking adds to the Jesus effect. He looks considerably younger than his thirty-four years. I meet with Becker at his modest, one-bedroom rental apartment in a high-rise at Yonge and St. Clair. He greets me at the door with an unexpected hug, and an offer of tea and toast.

Becker, an only child, grew up in Toronto's west end, near Lansdowne and Bloor. His father, Mark, was a master plumber who left his wife and infant son, returning to his native Detroit ten months after Becker was born. His mother, Lynette, a devout Anglican who played the pipe organ at her local church, raised her son on her own. Eldrich was a bright boy, an early reader who always had his nose in a book, but he didn't do well in school. He was easily distracted and had trouble focusing. The older he got, the less meaningful the standard curriculum felt to him. When he was fourteen, Becker dropped out of junior high, left home and began busking on the streets of the Annex for change. "I felt happy to be free of the brick building and out into the *real* school," he recalls. "It didn't bother me that I was homeless or eating out of Dumpsters half the time. Just the opposite. I felt ecstatic. I was playing music, reading a lot, learning a lot, meeting great people, sharing ideas . . . I'm lucky because I found the right way to live early on. And I've been living that way ever since." Becker smiles radiantly. His apartment is alive and green with dozens of houseplants. There are musical instruments of all kinds scattered about, and numerous books shelved in old Sealtest milk crates. There are volumes of poetry and philosophy—Keats, Kierkegaard, Plato, Thomas More. Another crate holds the *Summa Theologica* of St. Thomas Aquinas, the *Bhagavad Gita*; *The Essential Talmud*, and Augustine's *Confessions*. *There Are Men Too Gentle to Live Among Wolves* by James Kavanaugh lies open on the arm of Becker's fraying wicker peacock chair. He seems more like a genuine bohemian than the president of a corporation that held seminars, solicited donations and sold T-shirts, souvenir photos and DVDs to the tune of close to two million dollars in its first fiscal year. He explains that his role in the Institute was to "explore truer ways of being and share God's love with Seekers" (the official name given by the Institute to its followers). Administration, finances and all business matters, he says, were handled entirely by the other principal players at the head of the Institute: John Aarons and Amy McCullough—a young couple who lived across the hall from Becker. (Aarons and McCullough are no longer romantically involved. Both declined to be interviewed by *T.O. Magazine*.) Aarons, a twenty-nine-year-old art school dropout, befriended Becker and quickly became interested in his philosophical and spiritual views. He introduced Becker to McCullough, who was studying psychology at York University.

Becker tells me that, for several months, he acted as a kind of mentor to Aarons, who was undergoing a spiritual awakening. "He was a man divided," says Becker. "Hungry for God, but angry, confused . . . deeply wounded by what happened to his mom and dad." Aarons's parents, David and Voskie, died in 2003 while vacationing in Cabo San Lucas. The couple went swimming at Neblina Beach—a spot known for its dangerous riptides—and were pulled out to sea by a powerful current. At the time, reporters speculated the pair may well have been aware of the widely acknowledged risks of entering the water at Neblina Beach. Just a few weeks prior to leaving for Mexico, the couple learned they were among the dozens of victims whose life savings had been squandered by Paul Hagopian, a former mutual fund salesman at IGC Financial, and long-time family friend. (Hagopian, who had gambling and cocaine addictions, eventually pleaded guilty to thirty-three counts of fraud and served six years in prison.) Becker tells me John Aarons was haunted by his parents' death but was able to find solace through Becker and his teachings. "He was in the dark, and I helped guide him toward the light," says Becker. "I guess he wanted to share that experience with others."

Aarons set up a website and started postering the city to tell people about Becker's ideas. "I wasn't sure I was equipped to help a lot of people find truth," Becker admits. "But I thought John's impulse was generous and beautiful." Aarons's "generous and beautiful" impulse eventually netted the struggling artist and his girlfriend handsome salaries and powerful ownership positions in the burgeoning Institute (McCullough soon quit school to work there full time). Becker, who is listed as president of the Answer Institute, Inc., maintains it was McCullough who set up the corporation in the first place, and that she and Aarons ran the day-to-day operations. He tells me he is not and never was a "guru," and has no time for money, power or material gain. Instead, his only interests are "music and truth."

Eldrich pours me a fresh cup of blueberry tea and offers organic honey. He asks me about my life, leaning forward, staring deeply into my eyes, as if my response is of great importance to him. It's not difficult to see how one could become captivated by this man.

DREW WOOLLINGS WAS ONE OF THE MANY SEEKERS who became enthralled with Eldrich Becker. It was in the summer of 2012 that he first gained awareness of the Answer Institute. At the time, the twenty-seven-year-old Woollings was working as a temp, recruiting blood donors for Canadian Blood Services, and living in a rundown rooming house at Jarvis and Gerrard. He felt depressed and lonely. Purposeless. He was craving connection and guidance. That's when he noticed the posters the Answer Institute had pasted to the hoardings and lampposts along Jarvis Street. The posters included inspirational messages that seemed to speak to him, messages that beckoned with promises of spiritual illumination, healing and community. He decided to get in touch.

Today, Woollings lies in a hospital bed, with second- and third-degree burns covering 40 percent of his body. He spent more than a month in a coma and is now struggling to overcome the physiological, cognitive and emotional effects of the injuries he sustained at 81 Elderbrook on February 1, 2013. He is lucky to be alive. Nine of his fellow Seekers died that night.

Woollings, who was eventually employed by the Institute and became one of about a dozen insiders, recalls his first contact with Becker and the organization. "I went to the website they advertised on the posters. There was this kind of poem there about finding the true you and finding the true answers to your problems. And there was a place where you could comment and share stuff about your life. So I did." Woollings wrote about his frustrations with work and home, about feeling aimless and isolated. Within twenty-four hours, Becker wrote back, offering words of consolation, understanding and encouragement. Woollings felt Becker truly grasped his plight. A correspondence ensued. Before long, he was invited to attend a gathering—ostensibly the Institute's first—at Becker's apartment. "They had it out on the roof patio. It was more of a meet-and-greet than an actual meeting," Woollings recalls. "We just kind of said hello and chatted. I guess there were about thirty people there . . . John and Amy . . . Phil, Tyson, Wayne, Anne-Marie, Marina, Catelyn . . . Mindy and Alexa . . ." His voice trails off; all the people he mentioned—with the exception of organizers John Aarons and Amy McCullough—are now deceased. Woollings tells me he experienced an instant connection and rapport with Becker. "There was this incredible warmth coming off him. You could see the light in his eyes. And you could see he was a humble person who had really communed with God. He told me that God was going to liberate me and set me on the path to joyfulness. And he was right."

Woollings began attending weekly gatherings in Becker's apartment, which at the time consisted mainly of Becker discussing random spiritual concepts with Seekers. There was no charge for these meetings, but donations were solicited. Woollings estimates that somewhere between forty and a hundred followers attended each meeting, and that each individual donated at least twenty dollars, and often a great deal more. He says that it was a badge of honour among followers to donate every spare penny to the cause. In addition to cash, many Seekers brought Becker gifts of food, clothing, books and household goods.

One of the Institute's original members, and its largest financial backer, was Phil (Quan). It is difficult to determine precisely how much money Quan contributed to the Institute, but the organization's website shows that he donated at least seventy-five thousand dollars to its building fund, which was set up to raise money to purchase a permanent headquarters. When Quan was diagnosed with stomach cancer and grew too weak to attend meetings at the Yonge and St. Clair apartment, Becker moved the gatherings to Quan's home at 81 Elderbrook to accommodate his benefactor. Becker had followers participate in a series of "group healing and prayer sessions" for Quan, and it is Woollings's belief that these sessions were successful. Even though the rapidly declining Quan ultimately required a total gastrectomy, which he opted to have at the world renowned Memorial Sloan Kettering Cancer Center (a procedure that was successful—Quan was in remission from cancer when he died), Woollings assures me that it was the Institute's healing sessions that gave him the strength to travel to New York City to do so.

It was in New York that the fortunes of the Institute changed dramatically. That's where Becker, while visiting Quan in hospital, met the man who would become the Institute's first and most famous celebrity member—Xavier Raine Maddox. For seven seasons, Maddox played a detective on ABC's popular police procedural *Chicago Blues*, but he is perhaps best known as the star of the cult sci-fi series *Deep Sky*. He has legions of avid fans. A recent check on Twitter reveals Maddox has in excess of 1.6 million followers. When Maddox started tweeting to his fans about Becker and the Institute, urging them to follow Becker (who was also tweeting), things changed at 81 Elderbrook. "Suddenly there were a lot of people interested," says Woollings. "A lot more people were coming to the meetings, and a lot were just showing up all the time." The Institute started holding multiple weekend "seminars" and charging hefty admission fees. And that's when Aarons and McCullough took Woollings aside and offered him an administrative assistant position at the rapidly growing Institute. He would receive room and board at 81 Elderbrook, and a modest salary (twelve thousand dollars per year), and he would be allowed to attend all meetings and seminars for free. Woollings was thrilled to be able to say goodbye to his temp job at the call centre and join the inner circle at the Institute. He wanted to be as close to Becker as possible, and accepted the position immediately. Woollings's duties included making regular shopping trips for groceries and supplies, picking up mail at Becker's and at Aarons and McCullough's apartments (all of them were living at Elderbrook at that point), and helping McCullough prepare, package and send out Institute merchandise sold through the organization's website.

Other Seekers had been similarly hired on to assist with fundraising, crowd control, cleaning and food preparation. Woollings tells me that in addition to Quan, Becker, Aarons and McCullough, at least seven Seekers were living full time at 81 Elderbrook, and many transient Seekers would often spend a night or two at the home. There were people sleeping in guest rooms, the basement, the pool house, even the covered tennis court in the backyard. But the best guest bedroom was always kept empty and ready in case Maddox decided to show up—typically about once a month. Woollings tells me that when Maddox visited—usually alone, but sometimes with his teenage daughter or a colleague in tow—he was treated like royalty. There would be extravagant dinners with champagne and expensive whiskey flowing, private one-on-one sessions with Becker (often involving drugs—typically, psilocybin, cannabis or peyote), and specially arranged "therapeutic touch" sessions with one or more female Seekers, chosen by Maddox. (Maddox, who officially broke off ties with the Institute in January of this year, declined to be interviewed by *T.O. Magazine*. He did, however, issue the following statement: "While I have not been involved with the Answer Institute for some time now, I am, of course, deeply saddened to hear of the tragic events that occurred there. I send my condolences to the friends and family of those who were injured or lost their lives. I truly believe that Eldrich Becker and Amy McCullough had their members' best interests at heart, and I wish them the best possible outcome to this unfortunate accident.")

Interestingly, Maddox's statement doesn't mention John Aarons, one of the three principals in the Institute. I asked Woollings if he had an opinion on why that may be. He told me there was no love lost between Aarons and Maddox (who Aarons often referred to as the "dwarf star"—Maddox is five foot six). Days after Maddox broke off ties with the Institute, John Aarons did the same. Woollings believes both the Maddox and Aarons defections may have had to do with a love triangle involving McCullough. He says that on the night Maddox left the Institute for the last time, he witnessed an emotional exchange between the two men after Aarons found Maddox and McCullough engaging in a "touch" session in the outdoor swimming pool. (Woollings had been asleep in the pool house but was awakened by the altercation that ensued—one that Woollings says ended with Aarons storming away in tears.) The following morning, Maddox was gone. Woollings's fellow Seeker Wayne—who was responsible for updating the Institute's website—reportedly told him that McCullough had him remove Maddox's endorsement from the splash page that very morning. (Maddox had donated twenty-five thousand dollars to the Institute's building fund, and had been featured on the website, encouraging others to contribute.) All traces of Maddox were erased from the website by noon that day. He never returned to the Institute.

"THERAPEUTIC TOUCH" SESSIONS—Institute-speak for sex between Seekers—were a prescribed and integral part of life at 81 Elderbrook. Unlike many cults and religions, the Institute didn't really have a codified doctrine; there were no particular laws—dietary or otherwise—no rules on behaviour, no Creation story. A review of Becker's tweets and his teachings on DVD reveal a hodgepodge of cryptic New Age, Buddhist and Christian beliefs. But Becker did have strong ideas about touch and affection. He told his followers that touch was physically and emotionally healing, and that sexual ecstasy would bring humans closer to the divine. Often Becker's seminars consisted of entirely wordless, two-hour sessions in which he simply fondled a succession of Seekers while everyone else looked on. Group sex and orgies were commonplace and encouraged, sometimes involving as many as twenty-seven Seekers—Becker had a mystical predilection for the number nine and advised followers to have touch sessions with that number of participants, or with factors or multiples of nine. Becker told followers they would experience physical healing and higher religious states by participating in these rites. Woollings contends that the touch sessions cured him of chronic neck and back pain. He tells me that many Seekers believed themselves to be healed of persistent ailments as a direct result of engaging in these Institute-sanctioned orgies.

Drugs were also an important part of life at the Institute. In particular, psilocybin, which was heralded by Becker as a powerful entheogen—"our gateway to God" is what he called it. He regularly fed magic mushrooms to Seekers as a kind of holy sacrament during Institute ceremonies and rituals. But it was another drug that eventually captured Becker's attention, the one that was used on the night nine Seekers died: ayahuasca—"vine of the soul." Ayahuasca is a psychoactive botanical tea made with *Banisteriopsis caapi*, a vine found in the jungles of South and Central America. The vine is commonly mixed with *Psychotria viridis* (also known as chacruna) or *Diplopterys cabrerana*—tropical botanicals that contain psychoactive tryptamines, including N-dimethyltryptamine (DMT), a compound that becomes active when mixed with *Banisteriopsis caapi*. For centuries, the powerfully hallucinogenic ayahuasca brew has been used in the Amazon region for medicinal and religious purposes. Woollings told me that Xavier Raine Maddox had travelled to Peru to take ayahuasca. When Becker learned of Maddox's transformative experiences with the drug, he became intent on bringing ayahuasca to the Institute. Maddox introduced Becker to Dr. Peter Scheibling—an American botanist who had spent years studying with various shamans in the Amazon region. Scheibling had been a member of a small New Age congregation in Santa Cruz, The Seeing Church (now defunct), that used ayahuasca during its Sunday services. He knew where to source ingredients and how to prepare and serve the tea.

Scheibling was invited to the Institute at Christmas to meet with Becker and make arrangements for a ceremony at 81 Elderbrook. When Scheibling saw that Quan's property backed onto the ravine of Wilket Creek, he was pleased. It was the perfect spot to hold the ritual. He suggested the date of the new moon in June (the 8th) for the first ayahuasca ceremony—when it would be warm enough to spend three or four hours outdoors. But Becker was adamant about not waiting until spring. He felt it was important for the digits of the day, month and year to add up to nine. That left only four, rather imminent, options if they were to proceed within the next twelve months: January 2 (2013/01/02), January 11 (2013/01/11), January 20 (2013/01/20) or February 1 (2013/02/01). Becker settled on the first day of February, a Friday. When I met with him at his apartment, Becker told me that he hadn't chosen that date, God had.

As it turned out, February 1 was an unusually temperate day in Toronto. At three degrees Celsius, it was a full six degrees warmer than normal for that time of year. In addition to Scheibling,

Becker and McCullough, the following Institute insiders had been selected to attend the first ayahuasca ceremony: Chen Xi Quan; Drew Woollings; Mindy Markovitz; Alexa Hjorngaard; Heather Mitchell; Wayne Samotowka, Tyson Griggs; Catelyn Campbell; Marina Dwyer, Anne-Marie Zielinski and her son, Richard Zielinski; Steven Reimer; Perry La Farge and Moina Quinn. La Farge and Quinn, who met at the notorious Rochdale College in 1971 and made an NFB documentary about their time there, had planned on participating but ultimately opted out. I spoke with Quinn, who told me that La Farge (who is sixty-three) suffers from atrial fibrillation. He experienced a prolonged attack of AFib in the very early hours of February 1 and wasn't sure if he should risk taking ayahuasca (a stimulant) that evening. When Quinn woke up later that morning with a runny nose and a sore throat, it settled the matter. The couple would stay put. "This [the ceremony] was something Eldrich [Becker] wanted to do on a regular basis," Quinn said. "We figured there would be many opportunities to try it [ayahuasca] in the future. We didn't think it would be a big deal if we stayed home that night." Quinn pauses, then adds, "Little did we know . . ."

DREW WOOLLINGS'S MEMORY OF FEBRUARY 1 is disjointed and tinged with fresh grief. He lost loved ones that night, including the two women he likes to call his "brides": Mindy Markovitz and Alexa Hjorngaard. Markovitz and Hjorngaard lived with Woollings in the pool house and were his regular partners in touch sessions. Woollings speaks slowly and haltingly from his hospital bed as he tries to sort out the details of what happened on the night of the ceremony. "We went out just before dark . . . I guess around 5:30 or so. It was snowing a bit, but nothing major. I remember everyone was really hungry because all we had had was soup that day. But Peter [Scheibling] said we'd be very glad, and everyone was kind of laughing about that." Ayahuasca is known to be a strong purgative. Those who ingest the brew will often experience violent bouts of vomiting or diarrhea. Scheibling had put participants on a strict diet to prepare for the event. He also erected a ceremonial tent under a large, mature oak tree at the edge of the ravine in Quan's backyard. "First, he [Scheibling] blessed the tent with this special flower water that he sprinkled around, and then he cleansed it with tobacco smoke. Then we all took our spots and he blessed each of us with the water and the smoke. Oh, and he had music on . . . I can't remember what he called it, some chanting music with a foreign name [icaros are the traditional songs sung by shamans during ayahuasca rituals]. And then he gave us the cups to drink." Woollings closes his eyes and takes a few breaths before continuing. "I remember the first thing was just feeling really sick to my stomach, and then throwing up—we had these buckets to throw up in. And then I started to see, like, these weird kaleidoscopes of colour." Woollings tells me that's when he lost track of time. For at least the next couple of hours, he was entirely focused on the images appearing in his mind, and almost completely unaware of his fellow Seekers and what was going on around him. "I could hear things, I guess . . . laughing . . . people being sick . . . but my eyes were closed and I was just really concentrating on the stuff I could see and what it was trying to teach me. It was like . . ." He pauses, trying to find the correct words. "I don't know . . . It wasn't like mushrooms, where you're interacting with people, or where real things just look kind of weird or exaggerated. This was, like, way more powerful. I literally saw and became part of a whole new realm. One that's always there, below the surface, but I didn't know was there . . ."

Woollings can't say for sure how long he was in this state. He tells me that when the drug's effect started to wane, he opened his eyes and had a startling realization. "We were in the middle of this crazy storm and I didn't even know it. The wind was nuts, and the snow was thick and wet and swirling . . . it was like a whiteout." Woollings saw a peculiar sight then, coming through the snow. It was Becker, outside the tent, completely covered in mud. "He was shouting at us," said Woollings. "Something about all of us having to plant ourselves in the earth . . ." Woollings pauses. "He said that the earth wanted to share its power, and God wanted us to become part of it, to absorb it. He told us to follow him." Woollings and some others left the tent, trailing Becker into the heavily treed area just behind it. "I saw Mindy, Alexa, Tyson, Richard . . . I can't remember if Wayne came. Anyway, he [Becker] said he'd felt the earth's power and that we needed to feel it too. He told us to bury ourselves in the earth—so we could connect to the consciousness of all plants and living things, so we could receive the earth's energy. He told us to dig deep."

Woollings and the others started clawing in the wet, muddy soil, trying to emulate the trench that Becker had already made for himself. Woollings estimates that he dug in the ground for about ten minutes before lying down and covering his own body—including most of his face—with mud, dead leaves and snow. "I was really cold at first. And Tyson kept yelling, 'The Lord God formed the man from the soil of the ground.' But then he stopped and I forced myself to lie very still, and after a while I totally understood what he [Becker] was saying. I know what he wanted to give us . . . what he *did* give us. It was a gift. I felt it. The vitality of the earth and all living things were flowing through me. I was connected to all of it . . . and I could feel myself getting stronger. I never felt stronger in my whole life." Woollings smiles. "That power kept me here. It made me strong enough to survive."

THERE IS A RARE AND LITTLE-KNOWN WEATHER EVENT that occurs perhaps once or twice each year in Canada (on average, according to meteorologist Randy Maxwell). It requires specific elements coming together to make it happen, elements that are common in summer but extremely unusual in winter, even in the Great Lakes region, where it's most likely to occur. Thundersnow. Essentially, it's a thunderstorm with snow instead of rain—an electrical blizzard. It's the kind of weather system that can wreak havoc with its tropical-storm-force winds, ice pellets, heavy dumps of rapidly falling snow and unexpected electrical strikes. The mix of components required for thundersnow are extremely uncommon, so uncommon in fact that Maxwell estimates that fewer than 0.01 percent of snowstorms are concurrent with thunder. But on February 1, 2013, all the unlikely conditions necessary for this rare weather phenomenon came together in Toronto. It began with a low-pressure system that swept in from the Prairies, picking up speed and power on its way. When this trough of air arrived in Toronto, it surged skyward at thirty-five to forty-five kilometres per hour. The updraft met the city's unseasonably warm atmosphere (three degrees Celsius) and caused a powerful lift of warm, moist air. The combination of warm air hitting cooler temperatures higher up resulted in the freak weather system that slammed Toronto with heavy snowfall and gusts of up to ninety-kilometre-per-hour winds that felled trees and hydro lines and left twenty-seven thousand residences without power. But it was the storm's lightning that caused the most serious harm—three separate house fires in the city's north end, and the death of nine individuals who, under the circumstances, had gathered in one of the worst places possible: around the base of a giant oak tree.

BEWARE OF AN OAK, it draws the stroke. Like many old proverbs, this happens to be true. Oaks are more likely to attract lightning than other trees because of their high water content and deep central root, which make them more conductive and better grounded. Of course, nobody at the Institute was expecting thunder and lightning in the middle of winter. Certainly, nobody was expecting three hundred kilovolts of electricity to literally explode the tree under which they had set up their ceremonial tent. "There was this boom," said Woollings. "The loudest sound I ever heard . . . then pain—like my whole body was on fire—and everything went white." What Woollings heard was the nearby oak being been split from crown to root as the water content in the tree boiled. Those who had remained in the tent, directly under the tree's branches, were killed instantly. Those who had followed Becker into the woods to dig in the soil received the somewhat less lethal current that passed down through the tree and radiated outward along the wet ground—still volatile enough to cause severe burns or cardiopulmonary arrest. In fact, Woollings—who dug the farthest from the source—was the only survivor of those who remained near the ceremonial site (Becker left the scene; McCullough and Mitchell sought shelter at various points during the storm). When I interviewed Eldrich Becker in his apartment, he told me that God had summoned him away from the area. "It wasn't a verbal command," he explained. "It was a pull . . . like there was a magnet in my belly and I was being drawn by force along a specific path through the woods." While Becker's disciples followed his directive to bury themselves in the earth, he meandered off through the ravine, eventually making his way to the Sunnybrook Stables in Wilket Creek Park, where he was discovered early the following morning, asleep in the stall of a chestnut gelding named Billy.

Woollings, meanwhile, lay among the dead, unconscious in the snow—his boots blown off his feet, his clothes singed and shredded—until McCullough found him. Today, he is deaf in his left ear, his legs are paralyzed (doctors say this will likely be temporary), he experiences weakness and tingling in both arms and hands and he has burns to 40 percent of his body, severe headaches, dizziness, arrhythmia and significant problems with short-term memory. His recovery, if successful, will be lengthy and arduous. Still, Woollings insists he has no regrets and in fact would happily do it all over again. He continues to revere and respect Becker, whom he credits with helping him achieve a new level of awareness on February 1, 2013. He believes that God spared his life so he could continue to work for the Institute. "I can't wait until it [the Institute] is up and running again, until I'm strong enough to help Eldrich [Becker] spread the truth to more Seekers." He smiles, but his eyes fill with tears. "I just wish I could see him," Woollings says. "I just wish he could visit."

It may be a long while before the Institute is up and running again. And it may be never. In addition to ayahuasca (and its separate botanical components), when the police raided 81 Elderbrook, they found more than a kilo of marijuana in the back of the freezer. They also seized a number of jars and containers that were allegedly used to cultivate psychoactive psilocybin mushrooms. Eldrich Becker and Amy McCullough were arrested and charged with possession of an illegal substance for the purpose of trafficking, production of an illegal substance and administering a noxious substance. The crown also brought charges of criminal negligence causing death against Becker and McCullough. John Aarons, who moved out of 81 Elderbrook in early January but continued to collect a salary as the Institute's chief executive officer, has been named, along with McCullough and Becker, in a class-action wrongful-death civil suit launched by relatives of the nine Seekers who died on the night of February 1. The house at 81 Elderbrook, which was left (provisionally) to Eldrich Becker and John Aarons by Chen Xi Quan in his will, is also part of a separate legal battle. Quan's estranged husband, Mat Faisal, who has been alternately travelling and living with friends in the US for the past several years, returned to Toronto to challenge Quan's will and pursue marital rights to the estate. As a result, all of the activities and assets of the Institute have now been frozen. As a condition of bail, McCullough and Becker cannot communicate or be in contact with each other or with any former member of the Institute. Woollings, it seems, will not get his wish to be visited in hospital by Becker.

When I point out that his next face-to-face meeting with his spiritual guide may have to take place at the Toronto South Detention Centre, Woollings gives me a knowing look. "There was another son of God arrested and put on trial," he says, smiling. "And we haven't stopped loving him." □

SCULLY M (posted 4 days ago)

Am I to understand that this guy is seriously comparing his cult leader to the Lord? Looks like his brain got scrambled AND fried in that storm.

2-small 2-fail (posted 4 days ago)

Hilarious. Even the cults T.O. Magazine *writes about have to be on the Bridle Path.*

marsha c (posted 3 days ago)

What a terribly sad story, and what a shocking waste of lives. I read recently that only 21 percent of us attend a weekly religious service (down from 30 percent in 1985). It's clear that the waning of religion in our daily lives has led to a spiritual void, one that allows charlatans such as Eldrich Becker to thrive.

annon (posted 3 days ago)

I don't care if it's summer, fall, winter or spring. You hear thunder, you get out from under the tree. Sad they died, but c'mon! How stupid!

MOINA Q (posted 2 days ago)

My husband and I are members of the Answer Institute, I was quoted in the above article, and I can assure you that the writer, Griffin Hill, has either completely misunderstood or else wilfully misrepresented what our organization is all about. The Answer Institute is not a cult. Nobody took our money or fed us hallucino-

gens. It was entirely up to us whether or not we paid for seminars, or whether or not we chose to ingest various sacramental substances. Many of us, in fact, chose not to. We were never isolated from family or friends or deprived of food or sleep. Nobody ever told us how to think or behave. We were always free to come and go as we pleased. Only a total outsider, one who perhaps set out to write a shocking, salacious story, would regard us as a cult or represent our practice of therapeutic healing touch as fondling or "orgies." Countless people, me and my husband included, have learned a lot and profited emotionally, physically and spiritually from the warm, inclusive community of the Answer Institute. As Griffin Hill himself points out, Phil was in remission from cancer. His healing sessions at the Institute worked! I can tell you that John Aarons and Amy McCullough are both kind and caring individuals. And I've never met a more loving or truer soul than Eldrich Becker. Griffin Hill, in short, does not know what he's talking about. He has warped the facts in order to provide a titillating tale to readers. We are extremely disappointed in T.O. Magazine and will be cancelling our long-standing, thirty-one-year subscription forthwith.

~

Griffin

After the article appeared, Drew Woollings stopped taking my calls. I expected that. What I didn't expect was that it would be a problem, that I would still need him.

An editor at a small but well-regarded publishing house read my *T.O. Mag* piece and floated the notion of doing a full-length book on the Answer Institute. I loved the idea. Journalist/author. Author/journalist.

The snag was that I'd need a lot more material. More details, multiple sources and perspectives. And I had lost my insider. My key to the kingdom. Even offers to share whatever advance I may receive, or any future profits, failed to bring Drew around. He wouldn't respond to my emails or calls. And I knew better than to try to go through Mama Bear, who sent one rather succinct text a day after the article came out: *SHAME ON YOU!!!!!* I also noted the snippy missive Moina Quinn and Perry La Farge had posted on *T.O. Mag*'s website, so they wouldn't be letting me in any time soon.

Could I get more out of Eldrich Becker? Yes. Definitely. He was clam happy to be interviewed for the article and continued to answer emails and calls after it came out—but his responses were growing more and more erratic. He'd answer normally for one or two emails, but then get daffy as hell for the next. For example, I'd send a request for a certain Seeker's contact info, and he'd send back an entirely-beside-the-point proverb. I'd thank him, ask again for the same info, and he'd send a link to a song on YouTube. The more specific the question, the more obscure his response. Was he a total nut job or just yanking my chain? My last correspondence was a sensitively wrought, multi-faceted email question, which he answered with a photograph of a polar bear on an ice floe. Annoying. When I asked if the polar bear was meant to be him, he sent a link to an Emerson quote: *Standing on the bare ground,—my head bathed by the blithe air, and uplifted into infinite space,—all mean egotism vanishes. I become a transparent eyeball; I am nothing; I see all; the currents of the Universal Being circulate through me; I am part or particle of God.* Terrific. Bully for you. But obviously no help with my book proposal—the editor told me she'd want an outline of how I planned to "flesh out" the story.

I didn't have a plan. There was no flesh. Only the dry bone of Drew Woollings's experience. Most of the Institute insiders were dead. And the survivors weren't blabbing. Xavier Raine Maddox was unreachable. Even his publicist had stopped returning my calls and emails. Amy McCullough and John Aarons, the sources I really needed to tap, continued to decline contact—Amy, politely (thanking me via text for the wine or flowers or chocolates, and apologizing for not being able to help); John, not so graciously (the whiskey and craft beers would disappear without so much as a "Thanks, Bub" or a "No comment"). Radio silence from John-boy, and also from many loyal Seekers who were either steamed by my article or warned by compadres not to share.

It was frustrating. And discouraging. I really wanted to make this thing happen, but no matter how many times I twisted it in my brain, I couldn't figure out a way to tell the complete story.

I just didn't know enough about how the Institute came to be.

Oddly, it was only after I had completely given up on making the book a reality that it came to me, mid-lather during my morning shower. A eureka moment when I wasn't even trying.

I instantly knew how to do it. I knew exactly how to make them all talk.

PART IV

PART IV

Amy

How could this have happened? That's what everyone wants to know. And how I feel about it. Like that matters.

I don't really know how it happened. And obviously I feel awful. Especially for those who lost loved ones, and who will never truly understand what went on at the Institute. I wish I could change things. But I can't. I can't go back in time and unmeet John Aarons. As soon as my toes touched that quicksand there was no escape, just a slow sucking in. Even though my lawyers think I'll be fine—since I told people to go inside, and since the drugs were used sacramentally—it's still upsetting to have all these lawsuits hanging over your head. They say it could take a year or more before they're resolved. So I just have to live with this undercurrent of tension. It's not easy. It's affecting my health. I have this red stuff all over my hands. Eczema, the doctor thinks. From stress.

How could this have happened? I don't know. I wish people would stop asking.

And I wish they would stop asking how I, Amy McCullough, could have possibly been mixed up in it. That's what my parents and my sister and Barb van Vleck and her shiny new fiancé and all my old Facebook friends can't seem to comprehend. How could someone as *normal* as me have been involved with something as bizarre as the Institute? I mean, it's not as if my folks ever thought I'd be a golden girl like Allison, I've always been the screw-up by comparison, but I don't think they ever expected their younger daughter to be facing a raft of wrongful-death lawsuits and criminal drug charges. It's humiliating. Now I'm not just the dropout, I'm the "crazy sex-cult freak." Right. All I can tell you is that things are being distorted by the media, who seem to want to paint me as some kind of calculating cult-meister, while John and Eldrich come off as all soulful and genuine. I have to say, I was shocked to learn about John's parents in a magazine article. Whenever he talked about them it was as if they were alive and well and going about their business across town. It hurts that he confided in Eldrich and not me. I guess he never trusted me. But I can see why he had trust issues.

Another thing the media has done is make things at the Institute sound weirder than they were. I mean, I know we ended up in a strange place, but it was a long time getting to that point. And humans don't really notice things that come on incrementally. Think of Milgram's electric-shock experiment. People would never breeze in and administer a full fatal shock. But if they started at fifteen volts and then slowly moved their way up, well . . .

It's like aging. All the time there are tiny changes happening to your face and body, but you don't really notice them. You're not surprised every day when you look in the mirror. It's just another morning. Now imagine if your twenty-year-old self woke up and saw your sixty-year-old self in the reflection. You would freak out. Grab at your flesh. Refuse to believe. That's what the Institute was like. It got just the tiniest bit stranger every day, so while we did end up in a very odd place, it happened so gradually that no one really noticed.

Of course, the final night was the strangest of all. Our first ayahuasca ceremony. Anne-Marie's son, Richard, helped Peter Scheibling set up a maloca at the end of the yard. It wasn't exactly authentic; it was basically an event tent with a pitched canvas roof and open sides. Peter put sheets of plywood under the tent and laid Peruvian rugs and pillows on top. It looked really nice, actually, tucked under the giant oak, all colourful and cozy. Things could have easily gone smoothly. It could have been just another typically strange night at the Institute . . .

How could this have happened? How does any accident happen? Something unexpected occurs. Someone makes a bad decision. It's hard to think about with so many "what-ifs" swirling. *What if we'd held the ceremony the day before or the day after? What if we'd held it in the basement or the pool house?* You can drive yourself nuts with what-ifs.

I know I'm lucky to be here. And I find it interesting that I am. I mean, if I drank a full cup of ayahuasca, I likely would have stayed outside with everyone else. But something stopped me from taking more than a couple of swallows, and it wasn't the disgusting taste. No. It was an overpowering feeling that I should just have two big gulps. And it came to me as soon as I took the cup in my hands. I know it sounds loony, but it was as if the medicine had a message for me and I couldn't hear it until it was between my palms. Peter, our shaman, urged me to drink more, said I wouldn't feel anything if

I didn't finish it, but I refused and eventually he moved on to Phil, who was to the right of me in the maloca. Because he had been ill, Phil took only a sip. Scheibling told him that even if he didn't go deep into the ayahuasca realm, it would still be beneficial to have the power of the sacred plant in his system. I figured the same held true for me. And I did feel something. I started to feel very warm and relaxed as I watched fat snow-flakes drift down around the sides of the tent. The flakes left colourful trails, and I began to see bright squiggly lines when I closed my eyes.

I became hyperaware of the audio around me. Peter was playing Peruvian songs on a ghetto blaster. I liked the singer's voice, but the rhythm of the maracas was annoying. I'm not usually sensitive to that kind of thing, but it was scratching at my nerves in an oddly prominent way. Then I started to hear people retching, and that was vile. But after a while, something different came breaking through. Heather. I heard her crying, and all the other sounds faded into the background. It's hard to describe because it was one of the most profound experiences I've ever had. I felt like Heather's sadness was leaving her body and entering mine through sound waves. Her sobs were tiny flying things, moving toward me. The grief creatures entered my ears, squeezed down my throat and settled into my chest, making it really hard to breathe and giving me a kind of sonic sea-sickness as I took them all in.

At a certain point I didn't hear Heather anymore, and I got the feeling that her sadness was moving out of my chest and sinking down into my stomach. I was horrendously nau-seated, but at least I could breathe. I began to see images—a lot of swirling, three-dimensional geometries. Strange organisms began to appear: half-plant, half-animal beings that I understood to be guides from the spirit world. I felt deeply connected to these creatures and to the universe as a whole. I had a sense that ayahuasca's purpose was to teach humans about connectivity—it seemed like a fundamental substance, and I felt overwhelming affection for it. Then my mind started racing and I started seeing things from my past. I saw my family in all these different situations and started to understand things about our relationships in new ways. It was bizarre. I don't know how long I was immersed in this movie of my life. The last memory was with my mom and my sister. It was this day when Allison got to pick out a new coat because she got all As on her grade-six report card. I'd remembered it as her parading up and down the store in her leather jacket, flaunting and taunting because I didn't get anything. But when I was reliving it on ayahuasca, it seemed as if she was just really happy to be getting the coat, and she wasn't paying attention to me at all. And what I had interpreted as malice on the part of my mom (i.e., you don't get anything 'cause you're a dumb-ass) was actually her trying to motivate me. It was like I could now see it for what it really was.

I was kind of marvelling at this experience and coming out of the visions when I heard the first rumble. It was loud and angry, and it scared me. It also confused me. Could there be thunder in winter? Was this a real, ordinary thing or a once-in-a-lifetime message from the spirit world? I heard Tyson shouting then, something about the glamour of Satan, about rejecting the glamour of Satan, and he began chanting *yes,*

yes, yes, yes, over and over again. The second blast snapped me back to reality.

My trip was over.

I suddenly realized how windy it had become. The whole maloca was shaking violently. I said, "I think we should go in." I stood up just as the tarpaulin ceiling peeled halfway off the roof structure and started flapping crazily. There was more thunder. Closer now. I said it at least once more—that we all needed to go inside—but nobody was listening. Everybody was still deeply tripping. Could I have forced them all indoors? I doubt it, but who knows? All I know is that I suddenly got this intense stomach cramp, like my intestines were being twisted and my bowels were about to let loose.

As I hurried back to the house, I passed Catelyn heading toward the maloca, dragging Staci behind her. She told me they were going to check on Heather. I said I didn't think they should be out there—there were huge gusts of wind and it was snowing hard. I offered to take Staci back with me, but I must have looked dangerously stoned or sweaty or wild-eyed because Staci didn't want to take my hand and Catelyn didn't try to persuade her. Unfortunately, I had no time to argue. I rushed past them toward the house and just barely made it out of my snow pants and onto the toilet—they don't call it *la purga* for nothing. As I sat there, basically peeing out of my butt (sorry for the grossness), I had the strange thought that back in the maloca I had literally absorbed Heather's sorrow into my body, and now I was getting rid of it for both of us. When I was done, I felt very clean and calm and, I admit, virtuous. I drank some water, curled up on the family-room couch and fell into a deep sleep for what felt like about an hour but was probably longer. I have a vague recollection of being partially roused by a loud noise, *the* loud noise, I guess, but it didn't wake me. There may have been a bump in my sleep, but there was no consciousness. I swear.

When I did finally wake, everything was quiet. I checked the bedrooms. Nobody. Not even Catelyn and Staci, which was weird, since it was the middle of the night. A four-year-old should have been in bed. I had a bad feeling. I knew Catelyn was pissed about having to look after Staci and skip the first ceremony—Scheibling told her that ayahuasca is good for addicts, and she was desperate to try it. Maybe her braving the storm to "check on Heather" was just an excuse to join in. Maybe she was out there right now, tripping or being sick all over the place with Staci watching. Not cool.

I put my damp snow things back on and headed out across the backyard. It was still windy, but no thunder. As I got past the pool, I saw something strange, what I thought at first was the blown-off roof of the maloca, hanging from some high branches, but as I moved closer to the edge of the woods, my eyes started to make sense of what I was actually looking at. It was the oak—that massive magnificent old tree, gaping wide open.

The thing had literally split in half.

Then I saw the shapes of bodies, covered in snow, like those people buried in situ in Pompeii.

And then I ran.

John

I was awake when she called. Lucky for her, because I'd left my phone on vibrate on the coffee table. If some assclown hadn't pulled the fire alarm at 1:47 a.m., I would have been asleep and unreachable in her old room instead of eating cereal out of the box and watching a rubbishy Greer Garson flick on Turner Classic Movies.

She was instantly hysterical. Not what I expected, although maybe the phone spinning madly on its axis as if possessed should have been a clue. When I saw *Amy* on the display, I assumed it was a case of drunk dialling, and in the brief moments that it took to actually bring the thing to my ear I had already fantasized her plaintive, vodka-soaked plea for forgiveness and reconciliation, one that would culminate in me allowing her to come over and make it up to me with a tender though maximum-effort blow job. Wrong.

"Hello?"

"Oh thank God! Thank God you're there!" She was hyperventilating. It sounded like she was running.

"What's the matter?"

"Can you come over? Take a cab! I'll pay."

"Why, what's going on?"

"I don't know . . ." She started to sob. "Please! I'm freaking out. I need your help!"

"Just tell me what's happening!"

"I can't. I don't know! *Can you just please come?*"

"Fine! *Jesus Christ.*" I hung up, called a taxi and got dressed. Both elevators were busted so I had to schlep down twelve flights of stairs. Then, because of the wretched weather and fresh dump of snow, the cab alternately crawled and fishtailed its way over there, almost not making it up the hill on Yonge, and nearly killing us about twenty times. I was way more enraged than alarmed. I remember thinking: *This better be fucking serious.*

Unfortunately, it was.

Eldrich

One impulse from a vernal wood
May teach you more of man,
Of moral evil and of good,
Than all the sages can.

Sweet is the lore which Nature brings;
Our meddling intellect
Mis-shapes the beauteous forms of things:—
We murder to dissect.

Enough of Science and of Art;
Close up those barren leaves;
Come forth, and bring with you a heart
That watches and receives.

Amy

If I had even the slightest inkling that anyone might still be alive, I would have called an ambulance right away. Obviously. But I didn't get that close. All I saw were inert bodies, their forms smoothed by a layer of snow, like they had been dipped in wax. How could I have known that Drew was lying in the woods, still breathing? I couldn't! It was dark and I was alone and pretty much out of my mind with panic.

I called John. I did. I called the man who instigated the whole nightmare. I called the man who called me a "lying slut" and dumped me because I went swimming with Xavier Raine Maddox. I called the man who said he would make it his business to ensure I never saw a cent of Phil's estate, the man who—I recently discovered—succeeded in getting Phil to change his will so that the Institute was disinherited and he and Eldrich were instead named individually as beneficiaries. I called the man who, when he learned of my recent condo purchase, publicly insinuated that I'd siphoned Institute funds—which is bullshit; I paid for this place with my salary and bonus. Yes, I called John. And guess what? He came. Right away. In the middle of the night. He came when I needed him. No questions asked. So I'm thankful for that.

I'm thankful that, buried under all of John's anger, bitterness and mistrust, there was a flicker of something more powerful than hate.

John

I was shocked when I saw her. Emaciated and bony. Dark circles under frantic eyes. She looked ill. Anorexic. She threw herself into my arms. I was momentarily pleased, chalking it up to my absence and her guilt-ravaged heart. Wrong again.

She led me to the bodies.

Even before I got close enough to see much—Amy didn't want to approach—I knew there was only one thing to do.

"We have to call 9-1-1."

"I know," she said. "But do you think—I mean, shouldn't we . . . ? Do you think we should get rid of the ayahuasca stuff first?"

She said "we" but meant me. I guess that's why I'd been summoned.

"And say what? 'Um, yeah . . . all these people were just sitting around under a tree, in the middle of a storm' . . . doing what? Swapping recipes?"

"I don't know. We could say it was a sweetgrass ceremony or a sweat lodge or something?"

"Yeah, well, *I'm* not messing with that scene. And since you're afraid to even go over there, I'm guessing you're not planning to either."

Amy sighed. "Maybe it's not such a good idea."

"But, actually, it might not be a bad idea to get rid of the drugs in the house."

"You think they'll search the house?"

"I don't know. There are dead people here. Yeah, they'll probably search the house. And ayahuasca's one thing . . . but 'shrooms, pot and acid are something else."

"Shit!"

"I can't believe that tree . . ."

"I know. And there was a tent under there. With a wood floor and blankets."

All of that was gone. Incinerated. From the distance we were at, I could just barely make out the melted metal remnants of the tent frame, lying twisted on the ground among the bodies and branches.

"Who's out there, anyway?"

"Everybody!" she said, instantly hysterical. *"Oh my God, even Staci!"*

"Jesus Christ! What the fuck?"

"I told them to go back in the house! They wouldn't listen!"

"What was she doing out there in the first place? Jesus, Amy!"

"Maybe we should just leave? Pretend we weren't here?"

"A, I *wasn't* fucking here. And B, you're a little late, since I just arrived via taxi. You think there's no record of that?"

"OK. Sorry. I'm not thinking straight!"

"Obviously."

"Stop yelling at me!"

"I'm not yelling. You're the one who's yelling. Just fucking chill, OK?"

"OK. Sorry . . ."

"Just go to Eldrich and Steve's room and flush whatever you can find. Then go through Scheibling's room and do the same. Then call 9-1-1."

"What are you gonna do?"

"I'll be there in a sec. I'm just gonna . . . you know . . . have a look." Something in me needed to look.

"Really? I mean, maybe you were right. Maybe we shouldn't disturb them?"

"I don't think they'll mind."

"That's not funny."

"You'd better go, OK. We need to call as soon as possible. I won't touch anything."

As Amy hurried away, all my bravado seemed to hurry away with her. I thought I'd be able to approach and observe, but as I inched closer and started seeing details, I had to stop. For one thing, it was fucking scary out there—dark woods, howling wind, dead bodies (Scheibling, I'm sickened to say, had been stabbed through the belly with a long splinter of oak—pinned to the earth like an entomologist's beetle). But to be honest, it was seeing Catelyn that did me in. Or, more accurately, seeing her boots. I had taken note of these months earlier when she brought them home and modelled them for Heather. Stiletto-heeled ankle boots with a faux-leopard fringe around the top, a gold zipper up the back and a tiny metal heart to pull it. So awful. And she was so absurdly in love with them, high-stepping around the kitchen, but feeling guilty for buying them. All her money was supposed to be for Staci and Staci's bright future. She told Heather she was going to return them. But Heather told her not to. She said a mother had to take care of herself as well, that every woman had to have at least one impractical and beautiful thing in her wardrobe. I remember thinking, *Keep looking, babe*, and chortling about how happy she was to keep her ugly-ass boots. But that night, seeing them sticking out of the snow, all burned and muddy, with the zippers melted together . . . it just made me want to fucking weep.

I stumbled away from the carnage and sagged against a tree. I felt dizzy, like I was going to pass out. I pressed my face against the cool trunk and leaned there for a bit, deep breathing, grappling, not looking at anything in particular, just the dark interior of the woods and its dark shapes, when my eyes found and deciphered Eldrich's gruesome garden: heads . . . heads in the soil—one of them (Tyson), looking past me with a death stare, the mouth open in a gasp (only later did I learn of Eldrich's insane plan to dig under trees in the middle of a storm). A blast of adrenalin sent me lurching directly into a low-hanging branch. I staggered, bleeding and frantic, toward the closest shelter—the bubble. I had to get away. I had to get indoors. My overriding desire was to make it to MAMA, to hide inside and seek what Freud called the "soothing oblivion" of the womb.

Alarmingly, I wasn't the first to have that impulse.

As I neared the tennis court, I heard her. Faint and creepy. The heartbeat, the uterine *whoosh*, the soothing voice.

Catelyn's voice.

Mama loves you . . . Mama loves you so much . . .

The bubble was illuminated only by glowing glass eyes. I moved slowly closer, afraid to open the door on the womb, afraid of what new horror I'd find next. But when I finally worked up the nerve to approach and lift, I was met with a fine sight, one that made me sob with relief: Heather and Staci, in their matching green sweaters, curled inside like fiddleheads.

Asleep. Safe. Oblivious.

About to be reborn.

Eldrich

You want to know what is in my heart and I will tell you.

Faith. Pure and unyielding. Faith in God the Father. Not lawyers, journalists or judges.

I have come forth into the light of things. Nature was my teacher.

Nine hearts watched and received as God spoke his miracle into them. Nine souls came forth into the light and went gloriously home in the arms of God.

It was not an accident. It was not a tragedy.

It was a divine and wondrous event. A beginning, not an end.

My friends my friends my friends my friends . . . closer to God than they have ever, ever been.

I truly believe that.

I do. I do.

Amy

I'm very sorry for the Seekers who lost their lives that night. It's tragic. And horrible. But I know that, at least for a while, they found kinship and salvation in the Institute. I'm glad of that. I take comfort in that. For many, it was the first time in years that they had any kind of help or happiness or companionship.

The Institute *was* a positive place. People thrived there. I saw it with my own eyes. People perking up, getting stronger, growing . . . I mean, I know it wasn't perfect. Certain elements were maybe getting a bit out of control. And I'm not trying to whitewash how it ended. I'm especially sad and sorry that Staci lost her mom. I am. But there's no doubt in my mind that she'll be better off in the long run with Heather. I think even Catelyn would agree. She was terrified of falling off the wagon and causing Staci more trauma. Above all, Catelyn wanted Staci to have a future. With Heather she'll have one. And now Heather will have one too. She saved Staci, which I'm sure, psychologically, will help mitigate the pain of not being able to save her own child. And now she has a purpose— to take good care of Staci, which I know she'll continue to go above and beyond to do.

So maybe the powers that be, whatever and whomever they may be, knew what they were up to. Maybe this all went down for that reason. Maybe Staci is fated for some important task and she needs Heather to get her there. Who knows? I don't know. It's equally possible that everything is totally random and meaningless.

Either way, I'd like to think that, on balance, the Institute did more good than harm. And given that, maybe I shouldn't be sorry that I was a part of it. Right?

Of course, now I have to figure out what to do next. I'm not going back to school, I know that much. Trying to compete with my sister in academia no longer seems like a wise use of energy. I should probably just try to relax and take a few months to figure it out. It would be foolish to make major life decisions before all the legal issues have been resolved.

In the meantime, I've been feathering my nest. It's a one-bedroom plus office in a funky new low-rise in Liberty Village. It has super-high-end features and finishes, one and a half baths and a small terrace that can accommodate a few chairs and a barbecue. Oh, and the bedroom and full bath are upstairs, so the place feels more like a house than an apartment. It's really a gorgeous space. Even my parents were impressed. And it wasn't a bad deal either, considering it's a two-story. I love that aspect of it. I think a two-story is perfect for me. Best of all, it has an ensuite washer and dryer—full sized and never been used! So I don't have to share laundry, which is something I've been dreaming about for years.

The only drawback is that I'm the first person to move in to the building. I bought a model suite, which was the only one that was ready, and from what I could tell from the floor plans, the nicest. I assumed the rest of the units were close to being finished, but most haven't even been drywalled yet. During the day there are tradespeople on-site, sales people and prospective buyers milling about, but at night the place is totally empty. It's just me. And I'm not used to that. Apart from a short blip after Barb van Vleck, I've never lived alone. Ever since I left my parents' house I've had at least one room-mate. And, of course, at the Institute I was surrounded by people. Plus I had John. For a while, anyway.

It's nighttime now and everyone's gone. The suites all empty and dark.

But it's a beautiful unit. The bathrooms are finished in real Italian marble.

And I got a nice postcard from Raine the other day—technically, we're not allowed to be in touch, so no texts/emails. He said that when all the legal stuff is over, I'd be welcome to come down for a visit. So that's cool. I mean, I know it's going to take a long time and maybe nothing will really come of it, but it's something to look forward to.

I'm actually really looking forward to that.

John

You know what pisses me off? All the "act of God" talk. What happened behind Phil's house was not an act of God. It was an act of unstable air meeting moist air, followed by acts of baffling, unconscionable stupidity.

God did not "save" Staci and Heather. Heather was sensible enough to coax Staci inside when she heard thunder. Staci had been curious about "the lady" in the tennis court; Heather enticed her indoors by promising to show her the sculpture.

God didn't save. Common sense saved.

Art fucking saved.

At this point, I don't care what happens to MAMA. When I finish something, I move on. Artists are like sharks. Keep moving or perish. I'm onto my new project already. Heavy into it and feeling the throb. I rented a studio at Lansdowne and Dupont, and have more than enough for materials. The fridge is stuffed with organic cherries and grass-fed beef. The bar is stocked with Aberlour A'bunadh. I have all the time in the world to work.

So why I am so out of sorts?

I'm out of sorts because I can't sleep.

I can't sleep because I'm subconsciously irrational.

Intellectually, I know I'm not responsible for nine deaths or any deaths. I cannot and do not accept culpability for people's bad and stupid choices (i.e., burrowing under trees in the middle of an electrical storm). And yet I'm up every night with my heart pounding hard. It blasts me awake and keeps me that way.

My brain says one thing. My ticker says another.

One thing they agree on is that it's all very sad. I feel sad about those people. Especially Phil. Phil was a neat guy. Funny. Endearing. I really miss our daily confabs. Our *Storage Wars* bed-and-smoothie parties.

I find myself flashing on one particular night at the Institute. It was during our perfect summer. Before things went south. July 1. We had a Canada Day bash in the yard. Big barbecue. Lots of Seekers and friends of. Kids. Popsicles. Hot dogs. Sparklers. Much drunkenness and dancing on the lawn as the sun went down. Phil had the place wired for sound, and Mushroom Steve had made an all-Canuck playlist to groove to. "Sunny Days"; "Blow at High Dough"; "My Definition of a Boombastic Jazz Style." It was a warm night. Flowers blooming moist and humid, grass freshly cut. Everything smelled sweet and good. Especially after the neighbours down the street started lighting up the sky with fireworks, adding that delicious gunpowdery top note to the air. We danced and danced. Barefoot on soft grass. Kids darting around, waving their sparklers with hectic, allowed-to-stay-up-late energy. It was during the Alternaverse period, and there was a lot of crazy-ass strutting going down on the lawn. I myself was looped on tequila and jumping manically to Teenage Head's

"Let's Shake" when I noticed Phil watching wistfully from the deck stairs, smiling at the spectacle, too weak to join in. I pogoed over and scooped him into my arms. He laughed and hooted and threw his head back as I danced him into the centre of it all. The man was tiny and, at the time, practically weightless—an infant in my arms as I jumped and jumped in the middle of the madness. He couldn't stop laughing. Then the song ended and the first slow one of the night came on. It was something I'd never heard before (but have listened to a hundred times since). "The Valley" by Jane Siberry. Sung by k.d. lang—a live version. It was incredible. Otherworldly. I couldn't quite believe what I was hearing. That voice. That strong, clear voice, married to that lilting, gorgeously sad swoop of a song.

I danced Phil through it, floated him all the way through—dipping, gliding, soaring, plunging—while the kids swirled their sparklers and Seekers clung to each other, swaying. When the song ended, Phil sighed and rested his head against my chest. "Handsome, thank you," he said. "I die happy now."

Poor Phil.

Poor all of us, for that matter. Poor everyone, trying to make it in this hard world. Like plants in concrete. The tender shoots can't do it. They're not strong enough to push through. So they reach for anything that might help them gain purchase—drugs, God, booze, art—whatever gives them the strength to push through. But only the toughest weeds make it.

So far I've been able to find the cracks. But it's getting harder and harder. And sometimes, honestly, I just want to *not try*.

Sometimes, I just want to lie in the dark on a duvet that smells faintly of lemons, and have long cool fingers trail up and down my spine.

I really need to stop thinking about that.

~

Griffin

I had the solution. I knew how to tell the story. I emailed the editor and asked if I could please take her out for lunch to discuss it (rather than send an outline). She agreed to coffee. We were to meet at the Starbucks around the corner from her office at 11 a.m.

At 11:10 she sailed in like the *Queen Mary*. Large, steady, imperious. I bought her an Iced Hazelnut Macchiato and got straight to the point.

"Fiction," I said.

She looked at me with heavy-lidded eyes behind thick-framed glasses. "Fiction?"

"Yes."

She sipped her macchiato.

"You know what Ralph Waldo Emerson said? 'Fiction reveals truth that reality obscures.'"

A thin smile. Swathes of linen and sizable chunks of silver jewellery shifting, adjusting.

"It would be a veiled account of what happened at the Institute. You know, 'inspired by.' I'd set it in a different city, change the names and some details. And unlike the article, which was largely about one follower's experience, I would really get into the hearts and minds of the organizers and the guru."

"Hmm."

"I see it as a meditation on faith. What are we looking for in God? What does God represent? What are the things that humans need to feel fulfilled and happy? And what are they willing to do to get those things? I was thinking of calling it 'The Answer to Everything.'"

The editor laughed. "Well," she said, "with a title like that, you'll be obligated to figure it out. Your readers will expect you to know what it is. The answer. To everything."

I nodded, trying to process that. Then she told me that she'd prefer a non-fiction account (more marketable, etc.), but since I seemed passionate about the idea, she'd be happy to read it when I had a draft. She sailed out then. And I headed home.

For the next seventeen hours I barely budged from my computer, surfing everything from Aristotle to Krishnamurti to Martin Seligman to Epictetus. Philosophical treatises, psychological studies, poems, quotations, bible excerpts, TED Talks, etc. It was exhausting. Confusing. By the time the sun showed up, I had mega screen-head and felt giddy and stupid and no closer to my goal.

On a whim I emailed Eldrich. I said: *If I send one more question—my last, I swear—will you take the time to answer honestly and seriously (i.e., no pictures of polar bears on ice floes, no links to Blind Melon tunes)?* A few minutes later he responded (normally): *Yes. I promise. Send me your question.*

So I did.

And barely ten seconds later he sent a response. No words. Just one emoticon.

I guess I should have known.

Re: THE ANSWER TO EVERYTHING
Eldrich Becker
To: Griffin Hill

♥

Acknowledgements

Thank you to the following fine people:

Patrick Crean—my very wise and perceptive editor; Jackie Kaiser—my wonderful agent; Barbara Gowdy; Gil Adamson; Melanie Little; Lynn Crosbie; Iris Tupholme, Maria Golikova, Kelsey Marshall, Alan Jones, Joanna Ebejer, Emma Ingram and everyone at HarperCollins Canada; Kevin Connolly; Jason McBride; San Grewal; Hugh Graham; Kathleen Scheibling; Matthew Friedberg; Richard Kramer; Fern Sager; Betsy Aziz; Holly Kent; Ingrid Paulson; Judy Phillips; Chandra Wohleber; Stuart Ross; Denis De Klerck; Michael Winter; Alan Zunder; Ariadny Fragos; George Gooderham; Leah Simson; Robyn Friedman; Randall Cole and Max Friedman-Cole.

I am truly grateful for the support of the Canada Council for the Arts and the Ontario Arts Council.

Eldrich's entry on page 268 is an excerpt from the poem "The Tables Turned," by William Wordsworth.

Eldrich's quote on page 255 is from *Nature*, by Ralph Waldo Emerson.

John's photo-dissolving artwork was inspired by a piece I

saw in a small gallery back in the 1990s (either in Montreal or Toronto). Alas, I didn't take note of who made the thing, but I never forgot the brilliant installation. So thank you to the mystery genius artist.